ADD CYANIDE TO TASTE

KARMEN ŠPILJAK

Illustrated by
LUKA REJEC

First Edition, September 2021

Cover design by Miladinka Milic
Illustrations by Luka Rejec

www.karmenspiljak.com

Paperback ISBN: 978-65-00-26388-6
Ebook ISBN 978-65-00-26387-9

For those who eat the last cookie.

CONTENTS

FOREWORD

I set off to write my first novel when I was ten, unconcerned with things like plot or character or the fact that I didn't know how to write a book. All I needed was paper and Mum's typewriter. Yes, you read that right.

Since I played the piano, typing didn't feel all that different. I hammered away on the keys, sprinkling each page with a handful of clues and red herrings, then forgot all about them. About fifty pages in, I had plenty of intrigue, and dialogue exchange had over lavish banquets. I'm pretty sure there were plenty of cakes and strawberries with cream. After all, my protagonist and her side-kick had to eat. If only they'd be as keen also to solve the crime.

My love for food-related stories dates to a peculiar book I read at about the age of seven. In hindsight, the book of Japanese folktales probably didn't belong to the children's section of the library. The stories in it were bizarre, slightly frightening, yet strangely exhilarating. None of the other kids' stories featured spirits, ghosts or supernatural occurrences. I was hooked.

I can remember this book many years later, but I've forgotten what the stories were about. All except one: 'A Wife Who Doesn't Eat'.

This story follows a stingy man who didn't get married so he wouldn't need to share his food with his wife. When pressed by the other villagers, he said he'd get married only to a woman who didn't eat. His neighbours could have shrugged, but instead they said, 'Challenge accepted'. The word got around and one day, a young woman knocked on the man's door. She was beautiful and had a tiny mouth. Did she eat? asked the man. She said she didn't. They got married and the man's new wife indeed didn't eat. Was she what the man expected? Hardly. Did she have a sinister secret? You can count on it. Without giving away any spoilers, let me just say that the man learned his lesson. Because the story stuck with me, I wrote my own take on this tale and included it in this collection.

So, why make a whole collection of culinary noir?

Food and stories aren't that different; they nurture in different ways. For me, the two were always connected and I often read while eating. In fact, I still do. That is perhaps why I thought it'd be fun to include recipes for the dishes that appear in the stories.

And just what exactly is culinary noir? I hope this collection will provide the answer. Some of these stories percolated for a long time, others burst out kicking and screaming. Sometimes, they demanded a poetic license and the best I could do was direct them onto the page and leave them to their mischief.

One thing I've learned while writing this book is that culinary noir will make you hungry, so always have a snack ready, just in case. A careful reader might spot a recipe that snuck in while I was making a sandwich, offended that I didn't put it into a story. If you spot it, let me know what kind of story would be a good home for it. If I like the idea, I might write the story, too.

Please note that all the dishes should be enjoyed without cyanide. Most of the recipes are a variation of known dishes or my own creations. I added several recipes by my favourite cook, a wonderful woman who taught me how to love food and books: my mum.

I hope these stories give you as much pleasure as they gave me when I was writing them. Take care though, some might be spicier than they appear to be.

Bon appétit!

Karmen Špiljak

SHORT STORIES

THE ASSISTANT

You don't expect someone to die at lunch, especially not when you're there for your first meeting with a big client. My boss, Kevin, insisted we arrive early to prepare.

The restaurant was almost empty, a large, dimly-lit space that left enough room between the tables to prevent eavesdropping.

'With Oxley, privacy is a must,' Kevin said. 'He fired his last PR guys because they'd discussed details over the phone. On a train.'

'Let me guess. There was a journalist.'

'Isn't there always one? You can't be too careful when you work with a business like Bert's.'

We ordered water. Kevin, who hadn't eaten any breakfast, cracked a breadstick between his fingers and devoured it.

'I've heard he has a new assistant,' I said.

Kevin lifted his index finger and took a long gulp of water. I waited for him to finish chewing.

'Keep her in the loop, Anna. Assistants are the first to know when things go wrong.'

I eyed the remaining breadstick but decided against eating it so as not to spoil my appetite. As Kevin reached for it, there was a rustle at the door. We turned towards a large man in a business suit and a rather petite woman in long tweed pants and a silk blouse. She had a dark fringe and cat-eye glasses, the kind reserved for artists and people with strong opinions.

'Here they come,' said Kevin.

We shook hands and exchanged pleasantries. A moment later, a waiter presented us with menus. Unlike Janice, who studied the content with an intense focus, her boss flipped through the initial pages. It seemed as if the idea of having soup or a salad disgusted him.

'Ah,' he said. 'Roast chicken.'

'The best in town, according to the reviews,' said Janice, without diverting her gaze away from the menu.

'My wife keeps on nagging me to cut down on meat, but I keep on telling her that I can't look as if I'm on a diet, not in my line of business,' Bert said.

Kevin let out a polite chuckle. The waiter took our orders and returned with the drinks – water for Janice and me, coke for Kevin and a quarter of red for Bert Oxley. He cradled his glass.

'So, what are we doing about the leak?' he said. 'Those vultures can't wait to eat us alive.'

'We'll start with a press release,' I said, 'to clarify the leak was an unfortunate coincidence and you're investigating.'

'The news will go stale in a few days. The world will move on,' said Kevin.

'They'll run out of names to call me. What was the last one again, Jan? Satan or killer?'

'I believe they referred to killing in general terms,' Janice said.

Bert pulled out his phone and read out loud, as he scrolled down.

'Just listen. *Dangerous* pesticides poison drinking water in Taiwan.' He flung his hands into the air. 'As if it's my fault people don't read the instructions.'

He scrolled further down. 'Where's the last one, Jan?'

The muscles around Janice's eyes tightened. Slowly, she pulled out her phone. 'How long before AgroChems stop killing people?' she said.

Bert clapped. 'That's it. That's what we have to work with.'

'No problem,' said Kevin. 'We can spin this around.'

'I take it your lawyers are informed?' I said.

Bert licked his wine-stained lips. 'They're on it, alright,' he said. 'Bleeding me dry.'

At the sight of the waiter bringing our appetisers, Bert's mouth curled to the side. Foie gras for Bert, beef carpaccio for Kevin, smoked salmon for me and carrot and ginger soup for Janice. Bert pushed the pieces of salad to the side. The creases on Janice's forehead deepened as he sliced the foie gras with his fork.

'The soup looks nice,' I said to Janice, in an attempt to engage her. She smiled at me and scooped a few pieces of fried ginger off the top.

'We need to put an end to this cancer talk,' said Bert, with his mouth full. 'The shareholders want this taken care of, so make it your priority.'

'Absolutely,' I said. 'We did just that with Infestex. From what I understood, you only had one case, right?'

Bert Oxley swatted the air. 'Ages ago! They couldn't prove more than that. Of course, others saw easy money and…'

Janice coughed, as though trying to clear her throat, or perhaps, to cover up an awkward situation.

'Everything alright?' I asked.

She put one hand in front of her mouth. 'I'm fine,' she said.

Her eyes watered. She patted her chest with a deer-like gesture, elegant and on the watch.

'You sure?' Kevin said.

'She's a rock,' he said. 'Aren't you, Jan?'

Her face turned paler. 'I'll be fine,' she said, in a choked voice.

Bert pushed Janice's empty glass closer to her and I filled it with water. She emptied it in a few gulps and beamed at me with gratitude.

'Good,' said Bert. 'It's bloody impossible to find a good assistant these days.'

Perhaps it was a trick of the light, but the colour returned to Janice's cheeks. Soon after, the waiter brought our mains. He presented Bert with his roast chicken and rosemary potatoes, Kevin with steak tartar and fries, Janice with pumpkin gnocchi and sage butter and me with a mushroom risotto. We waited for Bert to start eating.

I was grateful for a few moments of silence, to enjoy the rich, earthy flavour of creamy mushrooms in my mouth. Kevin delved straight into his meat then took a break to fill up on the fries. Janice cut her gnocchi into tiny pieces, then chewed each one with pursed lips.

Bert moaned with pleasure. I avoided looking in his direction so as to gain some time to eat without having to talk.

It was a few moments afterwards that I became aware of a peculiar silence. When I glanced back up, Bert was glaring at me. His eyes were wide open and stood out from his round face. Perhaps some risotto had escaped the spoon and landed on me? I examined my shirt for food waste but found none. Bert's face was flushed.

'Too spicy?' I said.

Only then did Janice turn to Bert. The sight of him unsettled her.

'Don't worry, Mr Oxley,' she said. 'I'll get your pills.'

She reached into his jacket pocket.

'What kind of pills?' I asked.

'For his heart.'

Bert's eyes glistened with tears. He struggled to say something but couldn't. With remarkable calm, Janice searched through his pockets.

'Maybe he forgot them?' I said.

'I put them in myself,' Janice said and tapped over his pockets. 'Mr Oxley, where is your nitroglycerin?'

Bert again tried to say something but still couldn't. He

clutched his heart and staggered to one side like a drunk, before falling down. I rushed to his side and frantically searched through his pockets.

'Call an ambulance!' Kevin shouted.

Janice leaned closer to Bert. His mouth opened and closed, as his eyes darted from Kevin to me and back to Janice. All he managed to get out was a strangled 'Ssssh...' His eyes were shot with blood.

Saliva gathered at the corner of Bert's mouth and started to ooze. His eyes bulged. Everyone in the restaurant was looking at us, paralysed by the shock. The waiter informed us the ambulance was on the way.

Janice tapped Bert gently on the cheek. 'Mr Oxley? Blink if you hear me,' she said. Bert continued to stare at the ceiling.

When the ambulance took Bert and Kevin away, I stayed behind with Janice.

'I don't get it,' she said. 'The pills were in his pocket.'

'Maybe he lost them?'

She shook her head.

'I checked before we left. His wife insists he has to carry a spare, but he...'

'Did he change his jacket just before he left? Kevin sometimes does this,' I said.

'Maybe.'

Janice's face was pale. Her hands were still trembling when the waiter brought us some brandy. I downed mine and ordered another. Janice sat on the stool and stared blankly at her glass without touching it.

'I remember putting them there, before we left.'

'He'll be alright,' I said, but when my phone rang a few minutes later, restlessness nestled into the pit of my stomach. Kevin was calling to tell me Bert Oxley had died of a heart attack. Janice understood what had happened before I told her.

'I'm sorry,' I said. 'Will you be alright?'

She nodded, her eyes hollow, as though she was retreating into a blank space behind them.

'I haven't worked for him for that long.'

'Still, I'm sure he…'

They say not to speak ill of the dead, but I struggled to think of something positive to say about Bert. I signalled to the waiter for the bill.

'Janice, would you like to share a cab?'

'Thanks,' she said. 'I'll be alright.'

Despite my attempts to pick up the check, Janice insisted on paying for the brandy. She unzipped her purple purse, made of fake leather. As she pulled out her wallet, something rolled over inside her bag. I pretended to brush a piece of dirt off my pants so I could take a closer look.

There it was. A tiny bottle of pills with Oxley's name and thick black letters spelling 'nitroglycerin'. Janice caught my gaze and held it for a few moments. There wasn't even a hint of surprise on her face.

'You know what,' she said. 'I'd love to share that cab after all.'

This story has been highly commended on the Michael Terence Publishing Summer 2020 Short Story Competition and is published in 'All Those Things That You Never Thought Mattered', an anthology from Michael Terence Publishing.

SWEET LIKE BUTTER

The rain lashes the coats of those gathered around an open grave. Hardly anyone hears the priest. His soft murmur is lost in the plunking of the raindrops. People's gazes turn inwards, to the humdrum of their thoughts that drift like fog from places with little light towards those with none. Occasionally, thunder splits the drab skies with an unflattering flash of light. People's eyes shift in a lizard-like manner towards the young widow. Their tongues would stick out if no one would see them, but no one speaks. Only the middle-aged couple exchanges a few words, shielded by their distance from the grave.

'The poor thing,' the man says. 'So utterly broken.'

His wife purses her lips but says nothing. Her husband enjoys sympathising with strangers, much more than with those close to him. It's a special kind of blindness. She doesn't hold it against him but doesn't want to encourage it either.

There's little point in discussing things one can't change. When an old loner like Sam marries a pretty young woman like Ingrid, peoples' thoughts tend to sharpen against each other. She much prefers to form her opinions in silence, to give them time and space to thicken.

'Left all alone, the poor thing,' her husband says. 'Can't be easy, being new in town.'

She won't be alone for long, thinks the wife.

'We should invite her over,' her husband says, 'for a home-cooked meal.'

He says it as though he was going to prepare the meal himself, as if he'd ever made anything other than overcooked eggs.

'Let her grieve in peace,' the wife says. 'I'll make a casserole and take it over.'

Her husband opens his mouth as if to protest, but the priest has finished talking and the raincoats rustle.

People advance to the front to offer their condolences to the young widow and throw a handful of wet soil over the casket.

The widow hardly looks at them. Her chestnut hair sticks to her face like algae as she shakes people's hands in a robotic manner. Those who meet her gaze see that her eyes are brimming with tears.

'Sam was a good man,' people say. 'If you need anything, anything at all, call.'

Her chin drops. It's not so much their words as the shapeless shadow they push against her chest.

She doesn't look them in the eyes. She's not imprudent or impatient, just afraid to hear their thoughts.

The sun spun gold over the couple walking on the beach. The sand was a soft carpet sculpted under their feet.

'You'll get sunburnt,' the woman said, rubbing the man's red face. 'Let's find shade.'

'I thought you liked the sun,' he said.

'I do, but...'

For a moment, the glimmering ocean blinded her. She read-justed her straw hat.

'You could get sunstroke.'

He drank the salt off her lips. 'Worried, always worried,' he said.

She took his hand and smiled with her deep green eyes. 'I don't want to see you hurt.'

They cooled their feet in the shallow water.

'A little sun won't hurt,' he said. 'Not when we have the beach to ourselves.'

'I've never had that before,' she said, picking up an empty seashell.

'What else have you never had before?'

She took off her hat. 'A sunstroke on my honeymoon.' She put the hat on his head. 'Let's keep it that way.'

They rested in the shade of a generous tree.

'You're so beautiful,' he said.

She poured some water into their cups.

'Is that all I am to you?'

Her words pricked, but he didn't want to show it. 'Of course not.'

She turned her head to one side, as though she was thinking.

'Ingrid, darling,' he said, 'you are everything. Everything.'

She squirted some sunscreen into her palm and rubbed it on his shoulders. The sun started to set.

'I love watching the sand turn yellow,' she said and leaned onto his chest.

He inhaled her scent, the most intoxicating fragrance of his life.

'What else do you love?'

She tipped back her head. 'You.'

Gently, she bit his lips, then kissed him for a very long time.

Piles of folders and papers shield the solicitor from the tight-lipped woman who glares at him across the table. He remembers her face from the funeral. She's one of Sam's old friends. Only now she doesn't appear too friendly.

'That's impossible!' she says, pressing her handbag against her knees. 'Sam wouldn't forget about me.'

'What I mean,' says the solicitor, unfolding each word, 'is that Mrs Wringright, the widow, inherits all of her late husband's possessions.'

'Except for his books and records. He promised those to me.'

The solicitor opens the drawer and pulls out a black folder.

'His will states it quite clearly,' he says, moistening the tip of his index finger.

'Surely not. I've seen Sam's will.'

He flips through the pages. 'He updated it shortly after his wedding.'

'Because of her. I'm sure.'

The solicitor meets the woman's gaze for the first time since she barged into his office and demanded a meeting. Her right eyelid is twitching. Her cheeks are the colour of a ripe peach. He's seen enough people lose their composure to know she isn't the type. The way she clutches her bag with her freckled fingers, how her lower lip trembles, how her eyes flicker from side to side. No, this woman isn't angry. She's afraid.

He slides the will over so she can read it. 'Here,' he says. 'If you will, Mrs…'

'Peters. Amanda Peters.'

Her eyes scan the text once, twice, then jump across different spots. Her grip on her handbag loosens.

'You could dispute the will if you were a relative, but as a friend…'

'Not just a friend. We grew up together,' she cries out. 'I was his *best* friend.'

She checks the paper one more time and pushes it away.

'I'm very sorry, Mrs Peters. I'm afraid there's nothing I can do for you today.'

She twitches as though stung. Her pupils dilate.

'There *is* something you can do.'

The lawyer leans back. 'What's that?'

'Talk to the police,' she says. 'They'll listen to you. When they investigate…'

He lowers his chin. 'Investigate what, precisely?'

She flings her hands in the air. 'Murder, of course. What else?'

'You suspect foul play?'

The woman laughs. 'Suspect? I'm sure of it. She got rid of poor Sam and took his money.'

'I suppose you have evidence?'

'What evidence do you need? It's always the spouse, isn't it?'

'I'm afraid the police will need something… more substantial.'

The woman's eyes narrow.

'Look here,' she says. 'Sam was a creature of habit. He always drank his coffee black with two spoons of sugar. He's eaten the same brand of breakfast cereal since he was a boy. When his tailor moved to the city, Sam took the trouble to drive all the way there. He never went to the new one, not even once.'

'I understand your concern,' the solicitor says. The lightning that sparks in the woman's eyes tells him she isn't listening. She jabs her finger on his desk.

'He loathed seafood,' she says. 'Couldn't stand the smell. To think that he'd even consider swallowing a live octopus.'

'As I understand, the octopus wasn't exactly alive,' the lawyer says. 'It was killed shortly before the consumption.'

'It wasn't exactly dead either, was it? Since Sam choked on it.'

'I understand the situation is somewhat delicate.'

He considers explaining that the dish was perfectly safe, when prepared by a chef – he'd had it himself – but one look at the woman's enraged face knocks that idea right out of his head.

'People change,' he says and slips the will back into the folder.

'Not at seventy-two.'

'Even at seventy-two, to impress someone they love.'

He places the folder back in the drawer. Clearly, the woman has nothing but wild speculations. If she'd had proof, the police would have listened. Instead, they'd probably dismissed her, sending her straight to his office. Under different circumstances, he would have offered some tea and biscuits to calm her down. Having people storm out of his office wasn't exactly helping his business, but neither was wasting his time listening to her blabbering. He has work to do. Paid work.

He clasps his hands together and puts on a polite smile. 'I admit that your friend died under very unfortunate circumstances, but without proof...'

'She bought a new house, didn't she? There's proof for you.'

The solicitor bites his lip. No one could blame the young widow for wanting to leave the cesspool of rumours that was their town.

'Buying a house isn't a criminal offence.'

The chair shrieks against the floor as the woman stands up.

'Men,' she says. 'You see a pair of legs and your spine turns to butter.'

With this, she walks out, leaving behind a sweat stain on the plastic chair.

'What about the champagne?' Ingrid asked.

'In the fridge,' Sam said.

'You didn't have to go to this much trouble,' she said. 'We could eat out.'

He pulled her close and inhaled the sweet scent of her skin. 'I know,' he said, 'but tonight, I want to have you to myself.'

'I haven't been that bad, have I?'

She blinked in a way that made his knees soft.

'We've had people over every day for two weeks now,' he said. 'So, tonight, no guests, no friends, no drop-ins, just you and me.'

'And the chef, I suppose.'

He gave her a sly smile. 'I gave the staff the night off.'

She picked an olive from the plate, put it into her mouth and licked her finger.

'We hardly ever go anywhere,' she said. 'I wanted a little company.'

'I know, but I'm too old to entertain every day.'

She rubbed his shoulder. 'You're not old,' she said. 'You just lack patience.'

He chuckled, running his fingers down her bare back.

'I like it when you dress like this,' he said and wrapped his hands around her waist, 'for me.'

'I always dress for you.'

'Not always. When we're with others, men stare at you. You know they do.'

She shook her head, smiling.

'How about that young lad at the workshop? Almost cut his finger off looking at you.'

'Don't exaggerate. I bet it happens to all chefs, even the best.'

'The way he circled around you like a shark.'

'To supervise, nothing more.'

'He didn't seem interested in supervising me, did he? Left me to clean all that fish.'

She walked over to the window and folded her arms. On the other side was the ocean, dark, calm and tempting. So tempting.

She puckered her lips. 'I wanted us to do something... together, but okay, if you hated it, we don't have to go again.'

He kneaded her shoulder. 'I'm sorry. I didn't mean to offend you.'

'You said you liked the workshop,' she said. 'You even promised we'd try a thing or two.'

'So we will,' he said. 'Alone.'

She turned to him as though not quite understanding whether this was a fact or a promise, then skimmed the surfaces for a missed detail. In the corner of the kitchen stood a bucket covered with a wooden board. She walked to the bucket.

'Is that what I think it is?'

'Careful,' he said. 'I almost lost them once today.'

She lifted the lid and blinked at the pair of baby octopi,

stretching their tentacles.

'That's what you wanted, isn't it?' Sam asked. 'You've been talking about Sannakji ever since we went to that Korean restaurant.'

Her heart thundered. 'Are you going to prepare it?'

'Just like that guy taught us to,' he said, 'when he wasn't staring at you.'

'You sure you know how?'

'I chop off the tentacles and that's all, right?'

She buried her face into the crook of his neck. 'We should eat them right away. While they're still wiggling.'

'They'll be ready in a minute. Or sooner if you like.'

'No. Let's have some champagne first.'

As the bubbles danced in her glass, her eyes grew wide, so wide they couldn't conceal the excitement beneath.

'I'm so glad you could make it,' said the hostess and gestured at the suited men with white gloves who took their coats. Sam and Ingrid were shown into a room full of white orchids and golden baubles. Inside, a string quartet was playing *The Nutcracker*.

Ingrid drew in the scent of the room, seductive and sweet like butter. Her senses were well-trained to capture the faintest notes, like those of oysters and champagne, the taste of luxury and success.

'We almost gave up on you,' the hostess said. She nodded to the waiter, who brought a tray of champagne flutes.

'We wouldn't miss it for the world,' Ingrid said.

The first sips of champagne washed away the bitter memory of the conversation earlier that evening, of her tears and pleading not to spend another evening alone in their house.

On the glass table, the bone china and crystal glasses reflected the fairy lights on the ceiling. Ingrid's chest expanded, and for the moment she was inundated with beauty. This is my life now, she thought. The life I've always wanted. The life I've worked hard for.

A tray of meaty oysters was brought to the table. Ingrid squeezed some lemon over them and sucked them out of their shells.

'None for you?' she asked Sam.

He looked at her as if he considered her suggestion outrageous and reached for a piece of bread instead. A piece of bread, for God's sake!

Ingrid ate another oyster, then a few more, making a point of showing the pleasure they brought her. The hosts raised their glasses and toasted to the night and many more to come.

When, a few hours later, the hostess suggested they play a game, Sam frowned. He frowned a lot, lately.

'What kind of game?' Ingrid asked, trying to sound excited.

Sam pulled out his phone. Ingrid sat next to him and rested her hand on top of his thigh.

'Come on, sweetie,' Ingrid said. 'One game.'

Sam's face hardened. 'I'm tired.'

Ingrid massaged Sam's knee. 'You promised you'd try new things.'

More champagne was served on silver trays.

'It's a short, fun one,' the hostess said. She nodded to one of the servants, who laid pens and a stack of paper on the table. 'Take some paper and write down whatever you want to get rid of.'

Ingrid raised her eyebrows. 'What happens to the papers?' she asked.

'We'll burn them all for good luck,' the hostess said.

Sam tapped his pen. 'What if I don't want to get rid of anything?' he asked.

'I'm sure you'll find something,' Ingrid said.

'It doesn't have to be a thing,' the hostess said. 'Could be something abstract, like a diet or something that haunts you.'

Sam exhaled loudly. 'Alright, then.'

Ingrid couldn't help but glance in Sam's direction. His hand was trembling, so he wrote in big letters. With a grin, he wrote TRYING NEW THINGS, folded the paper and tossed it into a clay bowl on the table.

He kissed Ingrid's temple and peeked at her paper, but it was already folded into a small square.

'What did you write?'

'Won't work if I tell you, will it?' Ingrid tossed the paper into the bowl.

'I hope it does,' Sam said.

'It would be nice, wouldn't it,' she said and squeezed his knee.

The hostess lit a long match and let the fire lick the papers. Sam raised his flute. 'Here's to the future,' he said.

'It's bad luck to toast before midnight,' Ingrid said and kissed him. Sam's face lit up, as though his chest softened and something inside had unbuckled and spilled. He threw his arms around Ingrid's shoulders, decorated with fine cream silk and a diamond necklace.

'Can't be bad luck, if you're here,' he said.

She rested her head against his chest while her eyes stayed fixed on the burning scrap of paper. She imagined the letters on her paper blackening. There were only three. S would be the first to burn, leaving A and M to fend for themselves.

THREE ROSES

Around the same time every year, I go for a midnight walk. The day before Christmas, Ljubljana is like a new toy dumped on the muddy playground, abandoned. The planet-shaped lights seem desperate to inflict joy onto the empty streets. Defeat looms over the cobblestones like a broom, brushing away the last bits of holiday cheer and the final whiff of roasted almonds that lingers around the empty market. The stalls are folded against the wall, waiting to be taken apart.

Most people have scattered, gone to visit their families and feast on home-cooked meals. Those who've stayed behind won't go out at this time of the night, not unless there's an emergency. It's the sane choice given the weather, but I have my own ghosts to hunt.

Sixteen years ago, on a night exactly like this one, we walked these streets together. It doesn't take much to tease out the memories: the thump of my heel against the frozen tarmac, the scent of cloves and cinnamon clinging to the window frames, the need to wrap the warmth around me while comfort stays out of reach, tucked away behind the walls.

It's then that I summon the memory, the footsteps of two fresh graduates, high on wine and confidence, determined to find the one pub that hadn't turned off its lights.

The icy tarmac shimmered that night. I slipped more than once.

'Jeez, Barbara, take care.' Tina tightened her grip around my elbow. 'Don't make us look for a hospital instead.'

'The next time you drag me out, at least get me too drunk to feel the cold,' I said.

'Drag you out? Hah! You were in such a hurry you almost left without your shoes.'

I tugged at her sleeve to felt the soft filling of her winter jacket.

'Why do we bother?' I asked. 'Everything's closed.'

Tina lowered her chin and gave me that 'you tell me' look.

I turned away, afraid that if I said what I wanted to, if I let the words crawl out from behind my teeth, they'd fall flat and shatter like icicles.

'Let's try this way,' Tina said.

Dirty slush soaked through my socks. The discomfort was good. It kept my thoughts at a safe distance from all the what-ifs. The last thing Tina needed was for her farewell to become a drama.

We entered the old city market. The fog, thick like cotton, drifted up from the river towards the stone arches. Tina almost slipped but managed to regain her balance by grabbing my arm. I lost my footing and landed with a thump. Tina covered her mouth, then started to laugh.

'Sorry,' she squeezed through her teeth, 'but you flopped like a pro.'

'Don't just stand there.'

I extended my hand and pulled on hers. She tipped over and landed in my lap. We burst into laughter.

'You're not trying to pass on your cold, are you?' She scrambled onto all fours and pulled me up.

'It can be my goodbye present.'

'Stop with the goodbyes already.'

'So, you're not leaving?'

Tina punched my arm.

'Just exploring.'

The air felt like an ice blade sliding down my throat. Too much was squeezed into our last hours together.

Should I tell her, after all? It could be casual, unromantic, a few extra words that could slip out after I'd order the last round of drinks. She'd probably say something like 'I love you too, Barbs', then add 'You're my best friend' or something similar that'd fizzle out into an awkward hug. We'd part, as though my words carried no meaning and I wasn't trying to curve my life around hers.

'Let's go home,' I heard myself say.

Tina cocked her eyebrow.

'I didn't have you for a quitter. Besides, isn't a home just a place where you feel welcome?'

She took my hand. As we ploughed through the slush, I tried to imagine us as a couple on a casual night out. I squeezed Tina's hand through my mittens. She let me hold it for a few moments before letting go.

'My feet are freezing,' Tina said.

'Yeah well, I'm not exactly...'

She grabbed my wrist and put her finger up.

'What's that?'

'What's what?'

She pointed towards Ljubljana's castle and pulled my arm.

'Can't you hear?'

We headed towards the hill where the fog appeared thinner. The outlines of houses started to emerge from the background, as if drawn by an invisible hand.

'Still not?' she asked.

I held my breath. It took a few moments for me to catch a faint melody playing a few blocks away. As we walked, the melody became more pronounced.

'I know this song,' Tina said. 'My grandma used to play it.'

'Isn't it *Dream a Little Dream of Me*?'

'There must be a pub somewhere.'

'That or someone's playing it on their phone.'

We walked into a narrow alley. Tina stopped near a lamp, the old-fashioned kind that stuck out of the brick wall.

'It must be coming from there.' Tina headed towards a blotch of darkness.

'There's nothing there.'

The inside of my mouth tasted bitter. I didn't want to go on, but Tina headed right towards the dark spot so I followed. It turned out to be an unlit passageway that led to an inner courtyard. Tina propped her hands against her hips and nodded towards a building.

'See?' she said.

'Not really.'

She pointed towards the ground. Only then did I notice a dimly lit window close to the ground. The tainted glass was brown and green and had a picture of a red rose in the middle.

'A pub.'

'What if it's someone's house?'

Tina dropped to her knees and peeked through the window.

'You're so stuck up on homes and houses. What does it matter? There's a party and we're going.'

'How will we get in?'

'You *are* drunk. Come.'

She turned me so that I couldn't miss the stairs leading down to the cellar. I followed her down to a door with an ornate doorknob and a hand-painted sign that read 'Three Roses'.

'You serious about this?' I asked.

A sense that we were invading crept upon me in ways I couldn't explain.

'You want a drink or not?'

A flash of warmth gushed out as we entered. Inside, it smelled of beer and old things.

'We might be the youngest ones here,' Tina said, as we squeezed past the bar. People's faces seemed oddly familiar, like childhood mementos or pictures of people you've often seen but never talked to.

'There's nowhere to sit,' Tina said.

I glanced at a long oak table. A couple was sitting across from another man, all in their sixties. 'Mind if we join?' I asked.

'Please,' said the woman and flashed a smile with her kind green eyes. She wore a tweed skirt and a floral silk blouse that came together in a ribbon in the front. Tina wriggled out of her coat and hung it over a chair.

'What are we having?' she asked.

'I don't know,' I said and started to look for the menu.

'Over there,' Tina pointed at the blackboard near the bar.

'Can't read anything. It's too far away.'

Tina squinted.

'Lots of nice stuff,' she said, 'but I'm not sure the price is right. It can't be this cheap.'

I stood up. 'Let me check.'

'It's okay. Stay here and keep our seats,' Tina said and squeezed my shoulder. A jolt of electricity shot through me and it took a conscious effort not to react. I ran through all the clichés I'd been repeating for the last year. That it was better to say nothing, that we'd been friends for too long, that in a few days none of this was going to matter. Things might be different the next time we met.

As Tina made her way to the bar, I took off my mittens and my coat and spread them over a radiator. What I needed was to drink myself into oblivion and numb the stubborn kernel of hope.

Kind Eyes smiled when Tina returned with four shots.

'Blueberry schnapps?' I asked.

'Home-made,' said Tina and put the shots on the table. 'If you trust Milan.'

'The waiter?'

'The owner.'

I glimpsed towards the bar where a bald, red-cheeked man was wiping glasses with a tea towel.

'Making new friends already?'

The words came out sounding bitter, but Tina didn't notice.

'Cheers,' she said and clinked her glass against mine.

After downing the shot, I coaxed the blueberries out with my finger.

'Does it have to taste this good?' Tina asked.

'All I taste is alcohol,' I said. 'That bloody cold.'

'Well, I want to get hammered, before I...'

She paused mid-sentence, eyeing the remaining two shots.

'It's going to be a long flight, all the way there.'

I couldn't bring myself to say it out loud, to spit out the name of the wretched country. Tina wiggled her empty glass.

'It's Canada, Barbs. Not Mars.'

'Sure,' I said, 'I'll pop by for the weekend.'

'You could, you know.'

'Or maybe you could find a job that's a bit closer,' I said.

'Closer to what?' Tina asked.

Something shifted, as if a cold current passed between us. Perhaps that was why Tina turned to the other end of the table. Almost instantly, Kind Eyes met her gaze.

'When do they close?' Tina asked.

'Hardly ever,' one of the men said. 'Milan likes to have company.' Beer foam clung to the bottom of his walrus moustache.

'You come here often?' I asked, more out of politeness than wanting to know.

Kind Eyes opened her mouth but the man beside her was quicker. 'We practically live here,' he said. He had fewer wrinkles than Walrus Moustache although his thick beard aged him.

'Milan is like family. Isn't he, love?'

Kind Eyes beamed at him.

'What about you?' Thick Beard asked, rubbing his forehead. 'Don't think I've ever seen you here?'

'Don't be rude,' Kind Eyes said and flashed a smile. 'You'll scare them off.'

'That's alright,' Tina said. 'It's our first time.'

'We found it by chance,' I said.

Walrus Moustache tipped his head. 'Lucky you,' he said. 'Make the best of it.'

'Oh, we intend to,' Tina said and turned so she was facing them.

I hated the idea of competing with three strangers for Tina's attention. I pushed one of the remaining shots in her direction, but Walrus Moustache didn't get the hint.

'You don't look like tourists,' he said.

'We're not,' I said, harsher than intended.

'Not today, anyway,' Tina said.

They gave us a strange look.

'She's moving,' I said, 'somewhere far away.'

Kind Eyes arched her eyebrows. Did she sense the resentment in my voice?

'You make it sound so dramatic,' Tina said. 'It's only to Canada.'

'Canada?' Walrus Moustache asked. 'Now, that's something you don't hear every day.'

He waved towards the bar.

'It's not, like, forever,' Tina said.

I shifted in my seat, my eyes fixed ahead. Kind Eyes whispered something to the other two. Walrus Moustache gestured to the man at the bar and pointed towards us.

'The next round is on me,' he said.

'That's alright,' I said. 'Really.'

We raised our glasses and downed the schnapps. As I chewed on the blueberries, I noticed that two barstools had freed up.

'One for the road?' I asked, nodding towards the bar. Tina seemed reluctant to leave the company, but she took our empty glasses anyway and returned them. The masonry bar had a thick wooden top and an array of colourful lights flickering above. Beer and water jars hung off brass hooks in the back. Shelves were stacked with large mason jars filled with fruits and vegetables.

'Back already?' Milan asked.

'Milan, meet my friend Barbara.'

He nodded at me then turned back to Tina. 'You said it was your last time here.'

'It is,' Tina said.

'That's what they all say.'

'I will admit that you make great schnapps,' Tina said.

'The best there is,' Milan said. 'So, what can I get you?'

I felt a pang of envy at the ease between them. Tina had known this man for half an hour. Still, they talked as though they were old buddies. I, on the other hand, couldn't say the one thing I wanted to.

Tina mentioned my cold. Some moments later, a blond woman in an apron brought two barrel-shaped mugs. I stared at the cinnamon stick and orange slices floating in the crimson liquid.

'Mulled wine?'

'You don't mind, do you? Milan said it might help.'

I took a sip.

'And?' Tina asked.

'Burnt my tongue.'

'Oh, Barbs, I can't believe you're missing out on this. You'll have to come back.'

'Not sure it's my kind of place.'

'It's definitely your kind of mulled wine.'

When we'd finished our wine, I collected my things. I was about to suggest getting a cab but Milan and Tina were deep in a chat, like friends catching up. I couldn't understand why she wanted to hang around in a shabby bar. It didn't occur to me that it wasn't what she saw, but what she felt.

Milan gestured to the apron woman and she brought two more mugs. I arched my eyebrows.

'You can't leave without trying my hot chocolate,' Milan said. 'It's a classic.'

'I bet you say this to everyone,' Tina said.

'Only those who are about to leave,' he said and winked at me.

Tina took a sip of hot chocolate. Her eyes widened. She looked at me and at the mug, then took another sip. All I could taste was warmth and sugar.

'Do you feel anything?' Tina asked.

'Yeah, my burnt tongue,' I said.

She leaned the mug against her lips and closed her eyes. From where I stood, it looked as if she was smelling the chocolate.

'What do you feel?' I asked.

'Tickling.'

'What?'

Tina kept her eyes closed for a few moments.

'I can't explain,' she said, once she opened them. I took another sip and tried to pay attention to the details. The hot porcelain against my mouth. The tip of my tongue still itchy from the burn. Slowly, my lips went numb. Tina turned to me with her wide brown eyes.

'Taste anything?'

'My mouth is a bit numb.'

Tina smiled.

'You do feel it, then.'

I put the cup down, struggling to hide my irritation.

'Must be the heat. As far as the taste goes, I could have been drinking boiled water with sugar.'

Her gaze dropped.

'That's alright. You wouldn't believe me.'

'Tell me anyway.'

'It's like…'

She licked her lips and glanced at the mug.

'You'll laugh.'

'That's never stopped you before.'

She closed her eyes, perhaps to protect herself from my smirk, and took a long sip.

'It feels like a long hug, all warm and soft and a bit tingly.'

My knees became wobbly.

'It's quite sweet, but there's bitterness, too, like fear that it will all end,' she said.

I leaned closer as Tina took another sip. If I could, I'd have bathed in the scent of her skin, that familiar pine and grass smell, but my cold had deprived me of that, too.

When Tina opened her eyes, I got the strangest feeling that she could tell what was on my mind.

'Milan,' she said. 'I *have to* know what's in here.'

'I'm sure you do,' Milan said.

Tina put down the mug.

'I'm serious.'

Milan smiled and started to wash glasses in the sink.

'Are there cookies? I can definitely taste cinnamon,' she said. 'Chocolate, of course, milk, a pinch of salt, but there's something else, isn't there?'

Milan gave me a mischievous smile. 'Persistent, this one,' he said.

Tina folded her arms.

'I'm not leaving, till you tell me.'

'Who said you had to leave?' Milan said.

Something stirred in my stomach, like a poke into a nest I didn't know was there.

'I bet your friend here doesn't want to leave either,' he said.

I put on my gloves.

'I'm knackered, actually.'

Tina peeked into my cup.

'Aren't you going to finish that?'

'Have it,' I said, 'but afterwards, I'm calling a cab.'

Tina sipped my hot chocolate for what seemed like forever. After she finished, she turned to me with her big brown eyes.

'One last one?'

I sighed.

'Could we get two hot chocolates to go?' I asked.

'To go where?' Milan asked.

'To take with us,' I said.

'Oh no,' said Milan. 'No drink ever leaves the house.'

Tina put on her jacket but I could tell she didn't want to leave.

'Tell you what,' Milan said. 'If you like it this much, why not come tomorrow?'

'You're open on Christmas?' Tina asked.

'If you come, I'll open for you.'

'You'll make hot chocolate?'

Milan tapped her shoulder. She beamed at him. I got the strangest feeling that he was acting like the father she'd never had. They exchanged a few more words and I went out to call a cab. Once we got home, I collapsed onto my bed and didn't wake up till afternoon.

After a quick shower, I packed the presents from the artisanal Christmas market and texted Mum that I'd take the next bus. An urge came over me to get this goodbye over with. Ever since Tina had announced she'd be moving to Canada, I'd been trying to say goodbye. The closer the date of her flight, the more I found myself clinging to the sound of her footsteps in the corridor, the shuffling in her room, any sound that indicated she was near me. That day, though, I wanted it to be over.

I knocked on the door of Tina's room.

'Just a sec,' she said in a broken voice. A few moments later, she appeared, fully dressed.

'Going out?'

White flakes the size of oats were falling through a thick grey layer of smog.

'There's half a metre of snow,' I said and pointed at the window. Tina put on her jacket. 'I'll walk you to the station,' she said.

'You don't have to.'

'I know,' she said, 'but I'm going out. Some fresh air, hey?'

A chill crept down my spine.

'You aren't going to that pub, are you?'

She rubbed her hands together.

'I might check if they're open.'

'Isn't it a bit creepy that he said he'd open for you?'

Tina punched the side of my arm but she did it half-heartedly, as though she didn't mean to.

'Oh, come on, Barbs,' she said. 'He was just being nice. It's Christmas.'

We headed towards the bus station. A wet layer of fresh snow padded the path and muffled the sounds of traffic. Tina tried to lighten the mood by joking around, but a sense of distance already cut between us and moulded our sentences into a muted goodbye.

'Let me know when you get there,' I said.

'I'll call the second I get sorted out.'

We hugged. I got on the bus and tried not to look at Tina waving but I couldn't help myself. I waved back till she became a small dot merging with the whiteness.

Over the next few days, I kept checking my phone for the message. It didn't come. I told myself she was tired, jet-lagged, that she'd probably got invited somewhere to a New Year's party and maybe stayed a bit longer, made new friends.

When, in mid-January, I still hadn't heard from Tina, I sent her a long text. The message returned, undelivered. I called, only to learn that her old number had been disconnected.

I started inventing reasons for her silence because it was easier than asking questions. Honesty seemed like a stray dog, adorable from a distance, but if you came too close or offered your hand to pet it, you might find out it was rabid. The more I thought about it, the more I imagined what Tina's answer would have been, had I asked her if something was wrong. She'd wait a few days before sending a long explanation that she'd left because of me, that I'd made her feel awkward, that she'd always love me, but not in that way.

Come February, still no sign of Tina. I began to panic. On a whim, I decided to drop by Three Roses and ask if Tina had said anything before leaving. I entertained a thought that she had cancelled her trip and decided to work there as a waitress so she could get the recipe for that hot chocolate. It was already late when I circled around the old market. My memory of our route was like an old chest covered in cobwebs. I kept stumbling onto the same places without ever finding that blotch of darkness that had led us into the courtyard.

I told myself I was tired and that I'd try again later. In the following months, I tramped the city but I never found the pub. That autumn, I flew to Canada and checked the address Tina had given me. No one there had seen her. In fact, no one had ever heard of a Slovenian student living there.

I became obsessed with finding Three Roses. I started to take long midnight walks, sometimes after a few glasses of wine. I hoped being in a similar state would help me remember the way to the pub.

One time, I came close to what looked like the right spot. The streetlamp threw twisted shadows, distorting my view. Where I expected to find the passageway, was an old house. The tree and the lamp fitted into my blurry recollection or what was left of it. There was no passageway though, no courtyard and no pub.

I slumped against the damp wall of the old house. Tears, hot and sticky, trickled down my cheeks. Everyone I'd loved was gone. All I had was a handful of images, fading in my mind. The harder I tried to make out the details, the more they felt like an illusion. It seemed as if even the images didn't want to stick around but preferred to drift away.

Then, a light turned on in the house. I wiped my tears with my sleeve and looked up to where an old woman's face was disappearing from the window. Some moments later, a key turned and the door screeched open. Out came a lady with a brown woollen stole around her shoulders. She was old, but not frail-looking.

'I thought it was you,' she said.

I raised my eyebrows. 'Have we met?' I asked.

'You come here often, don't you?'

I was chuffed.

'It's not forbidden to walk here, is it?'

The old lady held my gaze, then slowly folded her arms. The skin on her hands was like cream leather stretched over thick blue veins.

'You're not looking for anything then?' she asked.

Her voice carried a certain determination which was perhaps why I answered her question.

'There's this pub I've once been to, Three Roses, but I can't find it. Do you know if it closed?'

She blinked. 'Oh, it closed alright,' she said. 'Long before you were born.'

My stomach knotted.

'That's impossible. I was there a few years ago.'

'I'm not saying it doesn't exist,' she said, 'but only for a specific kind of people.'

'What do you mean?'

Her lips quivered. 'It's like a song to them,' she said. 'Most other people won't hear it.'

An image of that night flashed before me, how Tina had heard the melody long before I had.

'Why?' I asked.

'Who knows,' she said. 'Maybe because they're lonely or lost.'

Nausea rose in my stomach. I remembered all those late-night talks with Tina, when she'd told me she felt like a tree that couldn't grow any roots.

'Are you saying it traps them, that place?' I asked.

'Think of it as a refuge. Most people don't want to leave, because they're afraid they'll never find their way back.'

Silence fell between us, crisp and cold, like ice crystals on trees. I dug into my pockets to stop my fingers from shaking.

'You've been there, haven't you?' I asked.

She reached for the doorknob.

'You should go home,' she said. 'It's starting to freeze.'

∾

My midnight walk is almost done. I ignore the slush that makes my feet feel like blocks of ice. Only Ljubljana's Christmas lights share my solitude, the planets and stars that are suspended above the tarmac. I think about them as I pass underneath, how we belong to each other, yet to no one at the same time.

I can't help but wonder what drove Tina to Three Roses that Christmas Day. Was it the sense of community, the feeling of belonging to a big family that she'd always dreamed of? Or was there something else, a fear, a longing, a need to exist outside her life? I thought about how Milan appeared to have guessed my thoughts. Could he have guessed Tina's? Could he had given her a sense of home?

As my socks get soggy and cold, I wonder what would happen if I found the passageway and turned the ornate knob that separates Three Roses from the world.

I imagine that *Dream a Little Dream of Me* would play in the background. Tina would sit at the masonry bar. The flickering lights would throw eclectic bursts of colour onto her silk hair. We'd hug. I'd tell her how I'd missed her, how I'd loved her all these years. She'd punch me in the arm, harder than usual, then tap on the empty barstool beside her. I'd order two cups of hot chocolate, no longer worried that our time together would run out.

DARK VELVET

All families have their secrets; ours has a curse. We rarely bring it up but it continues to exist in the shadows. Curses can do that. They hide and wait without ever loosening their grip on people's necks. You can sense them only if you unpack the small gestures and tics, the slight changes around people's eyes, the silences that fill the blank spaces.

After Nana died, things got worse, though. To begin with, we had to chew through thick legal waffle about Nana's bakery. We'd agreed that Noonan's Delights should be sold, but because of some legal hack, a Noonan had to be in charge, if only on paper.

When the solicitor asked us to provide a name, we all sat there and stared at our feet. Finding a new manager for the town's most famous bakery should have been easier than that, especially when it came with a substantial inheritance.

The solicitor gave us four weeks to find a name. If no one came forward, he'd blindly pick one of us, as had been Nana's wish. We said nothing, which in hindsight was probably considered agreement. I imagine we were all thinking the same thing.

Please, don't let it be me.

Subtle nudges, comments and calls were made to the extended family. I expected that would also be where the first rumours came from, but I was wrong. On Friday, I visited the town market to buy groceries. Elena, my fishmonger and ex-classmate, waved at me from afar.

Her apron and white rubber boots were stained with fish blood.

'Jim,' she said, putting on her rubber glove, 'I got fresh squid. Want any?'

'I'll take half a kilo.'

She lined the scales with paper and scooped the squid onto it with her gloved hands. Elena's ability to guess quantities never ceased to amaze me. After she'd registered the weight, she moved the squid back onto the counter.

'How's Alma?' she asked.

I found it strange that she'd ask about my sister-in-law and not my wife, who was down with the flu.

'Alright, I suppose.'

Elena started cleaning the squid with machine-like efficiency. Her hands acted as if they were operating on their own, twisting the cuttlefish bone before pulling it out, peeling off the skin and taking out the innards.

'Is it true, then?'

I lowered my chin.

'Pardon?'

'Your family business. Noonan's Delights? Is Alma taking it over?'

Cold air brushed against the back of my neck. I didn't want to appear uninformed, but I also wasn't going to discuss the curse outside the family.

'We haven't decided yet.'

'She'd do a great job.'

Elena wrapped the squid in two layers of paper and gave me the price.

'Anything else?'

I pointed at a handsome piece of haddock. She threw in some shrimp.

'In case you decide to make a stew.'

She bagged the purchase but paused before handing it to me.

'She wouldn't bring back Dark Velvet, would she?' Elena asked.

The name dropped like a hammer.

'Hard to know,' I said. 'It was the best-selling cake.'

I took the bag and paid. 'Will you call when you get that nice crab meat again?'

'As always.'

My chest was pounding as I left the market. I dialled Alma's number. She picked up after two rings.

'Jim!' she said. 'I was on the phone with Tania.'

I found that a bit odd as my cousin had never liked Alma. Then again, Tania could stay curious even with the most horrible relatives.

'What did Tania say?' I asked.

'She wanted to know if it was true. Of course, the solicitor couldn't keep his mouth shut. I wanted to make an announcement, but I guess I won't now.'

My heartbeat started to pace up.

'Announcement about what?'

'I'm taking on the bakery.'

'Are you sure about that?'

The sound of the wind crackled in my ear.

'I can't hear you, Jim.'

'Let's meet tomorrow for lunch.'

'Not sure I'll have time for…'

The wind in my phone got louder.

'Maybe coffee?'

'Coffee's good,' I said.

'There's a new café to the left of the main square.'

'Four p.m.?'

'See you there.'

I couldn't sleep that night. It wasn't just because of my wife's sniffling and coughing. I made her some tea.

'You'll get by flu,' she said.

'Then you'll make the tea for me.'

I fell asleep towards the morning and woke up around noon with a heavy head. My nose started to run. The morning tea tasted like water. I asked Alma to postpone our meeting. The next day, Tania called.

'Did you talk to Alma?' she asked.

'Dot yet.'

I blew my nose. My head felt like a giant piñata.

'You sound awful,' she said. 'Are you sick?'

'Flu,' I said. 'What did Alba say?'

Tania let out a loud gust of air.

'Couldn't talk any sense into her,' Tania said. 'She's taking over. Probably already has.'

There was a moment of silence.

'Did she say bore?'

'Something to do with her mortgage,' Tania said. 'Seems she needs some help paying it off.'

She phrased it carefully, so as not to offend me.

'It's alright,' I said. 'Will could't have kdowd.'

If the blood clot that had killed my brother had waited a few months, things wouldn't have been as bad for Alma as they were.

'Alma thinks that, because she married into the family, she won't get...'

My heartbeat throbbed in my throat, drowning out Tania's words. I couldn't hear what she was saying. Maybe I didn't want to, either. With a curse, there's a certain risk of contagion, that talking about it will poke the embers and rekindle the fire.

'Fabily's fabily, right?' I said.

Tania sighed.

'Alma thinks we're all a bunch of superstitious loonies.'

I bit the inside of my lip.

'You thidk it's too late?' I asked.

'To talk her out of it, you mean?'

'Yeah.'

'Would she listen?'

'I'b dot sure.'

An unpleasant thought passed through my mind like a cold current. Even if I managed to convince Alma not to take the bakery, we'd still need to come up with another name.

'People will get hurt,' Tania said. 'They always have.'

Tania sucked the air in.

'Are you sboking?' I asked.

'It calms me down.'

Judging by the sound of the lighter, she was having another cigarette.

'Alright, I'll talk to her,' I said.

'Good luck.'

As the weekend approached, I started to fidget with decorations and move around book nooks, as if to keep my hands busy.

'You shouldn't have promised,' my wife said.

'What choice did I have?'

'The rest of the family has no problem staying out of it.'

'Alma is family.'

My wife said nothing but I could tell she was holding back. Perhaps she was afraid that if she pushed me, I'd volunteer instead. It wasn't as if I hadn't considered it, but whenever I wanted to come forward, the words shrank in my mouth.

I was having my second latte when Alma's red Volvo pulled up to the pavement. Energetic as ever, she walked right past the sign put there by the guy who was painting the wall, then rushed under the ladder towards the entrance, choosing the shortest route.

'Sorry I'm late.' She gave me a hug. Her metal bracelets jangled. 'It took ages and I'm still not done signing stuff.'

My eyelid twitched. I stirred my coffee, even though I never add any sugar.

'Did you try any of the cakes here? I hear good stuff about their chocolate fudge.' She squinted at the menu. 'It is gluten-free, good.'

She ordered fudge. I asked for another cookie.

'So, the bakery is yours?'

She grinned. 'You're looking at the new CEO of Noonan's Delights.'

I undid the top button on my shirt.

'There'll be a grand opening on the first,' Alma said, 'so I have enough time to get things ready.'

'Alma…'

Once more, words got stuck in my throat. Alma took a long sip of her coffee.

'I hope you didn't ask me here to talk me out of it,' she said.

'We're worried, that's all.'

'About what?'

I pressed my lips together.

'I know what I'm doing, Jim. I have an MBA.'

'It's not about that.'

I stared at my plate. How could I explain the power of the curse without naming it? Alma seemed to have guessed my thoughts.

'You're not talking about the stupid curse?'

'It's not stupid.'

'It's also not real,' she said. 'You must know that, on some level.'

'Things have happened,' I said.

'You mean when your grandma lost her taste?'

'She never got it back.'

'Will said it was a short-circuit in her brain.'

'Yes, but it's more than that. It's been around for…'

Something rattled near the bar. I glanced at the waiter, who was emptying the tipping jar onto the counter. My face broke out in sweat.

'Are you worried about the cake?' Alma asked. 'The blood orange one?'

'You can't sell that cake, Alma.'

'Why the hell not? It brought your family a fortune. Without it…'

She paused mid-sentence as the waiter brought her fudge and my cookie. After the waiter left, Alma stared at the fudge for a few moments, then dug her fork into it and ate a bite. She scribbled a few things on the napkin. It said chocolate, salt, vanilla, avocado and strawberries.

'Will told me the story when we met,' she said.

I broke my cookie in half. The thought of eating it filled me with nausea, though. I doubted I'd be able to finish my coffee.

'Something about blood and revenge. I told him he could make a trashy movie if he added a zombie or two. He laughed about it,' Alma said.

How does one argue with a dead person's words? Will would have said anything to stop her from thinking he was part of a crazy family.

'It's much older than Nana. How much did Will tell you?'

'He said a hundred years?'

'Over a thousand.'

Alma put down her fork.

'Fine, so tell me,' she said. 'Because I'd like to understand why everyone gets so shit-faced when someone mentions Dark Velvet.'

The cookie fell apart in my hands. I stuffed a piece into my mouth but it tasted like plywood.

'For starters, you should know that Nana didn't only lose her taste. She also lost her husband.'

'He didn't die, did he, though? He left.'

'You lost Will. There's a history of… such losses.'

'Don't be stupid, Jim. If Will had gone to the doctor sooner, he'd still be here. People die. It's normal.'

'In our family, people die a bit more often. You'll notice that it tends to be one of the couple, not the kids.'

'Are you saying your family is cursed?'

'You don't believe me.'

'I didn't say that. I just don't see any proof. People dying or leaving their spouses hardly counts as evidence.'

Despite finishing all my water, my mouth felt dry.

'Did Will say anything about where it came from?'

Alma considered this, then ate more fudge. I pushed my cookie aside.

'The curse, you mean? No, he didn't.'

'You have to promise that if I tell you…'

'If you tell me? Oh, please. What do you want me to do, sign something in blood?'

'You can't discuss this with anyone, Alma. Not outside the immediate family.'

'What do you think I'll do? Go to a newspaper and say: please write about my cursed cake?'

'You've got to promise.'

She finished her fudge and put down the fork. 'I promise.'

Pressure started to build up in my forehead. I drew in a long breath. Alma folded her hands together.

'Please don't start with once upon a time,' she said.

The back of my throat tickled. 'This is all a joke to you.'

Alma checked the time.

'Go on,' she said. 'I'll have to leave in a bit.'

The tickle built into a cough. I held up the empty water bottle and ordered another one. I drank half of it in long gulps till the cough settled. Still, my voice came out choked.

'The first cake had real blood in it,' I said.

Alma smiled at me, as if she expected I was joking. She cocked an eyebrow.

'You're serious, aren't you?'

'It was a revenge. A woman's lover went off with someone else and got them pregnant. As you can imagine, there weren't many options, back then.'

'I suppose he married the pregnant woman?'

'He did. His ex-lover brought the cake to the wedding. It was meant as a present.'

'I assume the blood inside the cake was hers.'

'The spell worked. The bride died in childbirth.'

'Not so unusual back then, was it? I mean, even these days…
you need facilities, doctors. She could have been unlucky.'

'The man died soon afterwards in an accident. So, the baby
was left with the grandmother.'

'Is that it?'

'Not exactly. When the grandmother found out about the cake,
she swore revenge.'

Alma rolled her eyes.

'I have to say, this does sound a bit thick.'

'She found someone who knew about curses and put one on
the baker.'

'So she'd never bake again?'

I clutched her hand. She twitched as she looked me in the eyes.

'That she'd never find love or happiness. None of her children,
either.'

Alma pulled her hand away. 'This makes no sense. A cake with
blood?'

'They substituted blood orange for it.'

'But why? Who'd want to eat that?'

'You'd be surprised how many people wanted it, once the
story got out. The woman who made it made a fortune.'

'So, wasn't she happy?'

'The recipe was the one thing that kept them going.'

The chatter and clatter cloaked our silence. Alma gestured for
the bill.

'If all that was true, how come you're happily married?' she
asked.

'Mum had me before she married my stepfather. He insisted I
take the name, so…'

'So what? I also married in and took the name. How is this any
different?'

'You'll probably be fine, if you don't put the cake back on the
menu.'

'Did you ever try it? Will said it was very good.'

'I had a small piece when I was a kid. Had to steal it because Nana wouldn't allow us to have any.'

Alma shook her head.

'I won't have any, either, will I? Because of the gluten.'

'You'd be selling it, though.'

Alma stared ahead blankly for a moment, then took her purse.

'It's not that I don't appreciate your concern,' she said, 'but I've got two kids in high school. I need the money, Jim.'

'We could set up a fund. I could ask the family to contribute.'

She frowned.

'A fund? What am I? A fucking beggar?'

The waiter handed Alma the bill. She took out her credit card.

'Let me take this, please,' I said.

She handed her card to the waiter.

'I can still afford to buy people coffee.'

She stood up and pressed her cheek against mine. 'Take care,' she said, 'and please, don't worry about me.'

'At least let me help out with the preparations.'

'I'll call if I need anything, alright?'

She had to walk around the ladder because of a mime artist blocking her way. Once she got into her red Volvo, she sped onto the road.

That night, I replayed the conversation with Alma in my head. Could I have said anything different and made her change her mind? I wasn't sure. The nervous ticking in my gut told me I should have tried harder.

'How did it go?' my wife asked.

'It didn't,' I said.

'What about the cake?'

I shrugged.

Over the next days, I talked to Tania and the other cousins. Everyone agreed that someone should talk to Alma again, but everyone also agreed that it shouldn't be them. They suggested I talk to the solicitor and get Alma into a legal bind that would forbid her from making the cake, but the solicitor wasn't having any of it.

After some dawdling, I called Alma.

'Ready for the grand opening?' I asked.

'Almost,' she said. 'Minor issues with the staff.'

'What happened?'

Alma exhaled loudly.

'It's more about what didn't happen. I've been ill for days because no one else wants to sample the freaking cake.'

'You made it, then?'

'Honestly, I don't see what the big deal is. It's not exactly mind-blowing.'

'Have you tried it?'

'I had to, didn't I? Now, I can't stop scratching my face.'

'You could have called.'

Alma clicked her tongue.

'Yeah, after that speech you gave me the other day. Sure. I'd say, come and try the cake that'll bleed happiness out of your life.'

'I still remember how it tasted.'

Something rustled on the other end of the line.

'If you want to, the last batch has just come out. I'm pretty sure something is missing, though.'

An idea flashed in my mind. I'd meet Alma and pretend to eat the cake. Then, I'd tell her that something was indeed missing and Nana had probably taken it out of the recipe. People would notice and tank the sales, so it would be better to put it on hold for the time being.

'I'm free now,' I said. 'I could come over.'

There was a pause.

'The cake has to cool down and I need to pop over to the pharmacy. My head feels as if it's going to blow up. How about in an hour or so?'

My wife frowned when I explained my plan. She kneaded my shoulder for some time, as if she wanted to stop me from leaving.

The motorway was busy, as always on Fridays and traffic

started to slow down close to the exit, finally coming to a stop. Drivers left their cars to stretch their legs. One of them went for a stroll towards the front of the queue. I stopped him on his return.

'What's going on?' I asked.

'Some idiot came in the wrong way,' he said. 'They're still cleaning up.'

He offered me a cigarette. I glanced at his manicured hands and shook my head. He took one and lit it.

'Any idea how long it will take?' I asked.

He inhaled with a hiss.

'They've scraped the driver up already. It's just the rest that needs to be picked up now.'

The headache intensified.

'Here,' he said, pulling his phone out and showing me a photo.

Despite my intentions, I looked at it. Pieces of car were scattered all over the road. What remained had been loaded onto a tow-truck. My gut twisted. The shrivelled metal looked like a red rose with torn petals.

The man flicked the ash off his cigarette.

'A pity to ruin an Acura,' he said. 'It's a good car.'

My ribs felt as if they were shrinking, the bones stabbing into my insides. I pressed my hand against my chest.

'It's not an Acura, it's a Volvo,' I said in a cracked voice.

The man pinched the image to enlarge a bent wheel rim on the grass. He gave me an impish smile.

'How did you know?'

A DAMNED FINE COOK

My throat knots as I stop in front of Ula's door. The years haven't been kind to the brown doormat that now spells 'Wel me' instead of 'Welcome'. Ula's name is not on the door, as expected, but there's a stripe of black plastic with her initials above the doorbell.

I put down my suitcase. What exactly will I say? Twelve years ago, we were flatmates. Afterwards, she moved out and we started chasing jobs, careers and relationships. Saying we lost touch would be correct, but not entirely honest. How do you stay in touch with people who lock themselves into their lives?

I ring the doorbell with my clammy fingers. Music is playing in the background. I can hear the faint shuffle of someone's feet. Will she even answer?

Once more, I check my phone for a reply. My message to Ula was delivered but not read. I hold my breath and ring again, this time twice.

There's a rustle, then the music pauses. The footsteps circle around the room. What if she's not alone? I notice a change in the light as someone is checking the spy-hole. The keys rattle.

'Sarah?'

Ula says this as if unsure it's really me.

'I'm so sorry to drop in like this,' I say.

Her hair is short and frisky, her cheeks slightly blushed. She's wearing long black leggings and a stretched T-shirt that makes her biceps stick out.

'I've tried calling,' I say, as if this is an explanation.

She tilts her head and blinks. Then, her face lights up. 'Oh, that was you,' she says, smiling. 'I thought it was marketing. They like to use different numbers.'

The way she loiters in the doorway makes me think she has company. I haven't counted on that.

'I suppose you haven't seen my messages, either?'

'My phone is upstairs, charging. What is it? Nothing wrong, I hope?'

'I wasn't sure you still lived here,' I say. Ula glances at the suitcase by my side. 'My hotel messed up. I tried to find another one but they're all booked out.'

'It's the wedding season.'

'Do you know a hostel or a room I could rent for one night?' I ask.

'A hostel? You can't be serious.'

She lets go of the door so it swings open.

'Why don't you stay in my guest room?

My shoulders drop. 'I'd hate to be in your way.'

'Don't be silly,' she says. 'It'll be good to have some company.'

I drag my suitcase inside, trying to conceal the excitement over my plan working out.

'What's the occasion?' Ula asks.

'Work. I've got an interview at half past six.'

'In the morning?'

'It's the only time they could squeeze me in.'

'You sure your editor isn't punishing you for something?'

I chuckle.

'Not impossible.'

Ula's living room is stylish but scarcely furnished. There is a single cabinet with a few books arranged for display. I immediately pick up on Hemingway, Dostoevsky and Sun Tzu. I try to remember if I ever saw Ula reading something that wasn't a cook-book, but I can't.

'I hope you don't mind a bit of mess,' Ula says. 'My cleaner went home. Family emergency.'

I hide my relief behind a smile. 'What mess?'

'Here,' Ula says, reaching for my suitcase. 'Let me take this.'

Before I can protest, she lifts the suitcase and carries it inside as if it was a tin of beans.

'Let me clear out my junk and get things ready,' she says and takes my suitcase upstairs.

As I wait in the living room, things rattle and shift on the upper floor. By the sound of it, she's not only tidying up, but reorganising the whole room. I wait a few beats, then head to the kitchen.

First, I inspect the cupboards. Plain white plates, stacked and arranged by size. Generic, cream-coloured mugs, the type they use at meetings. The drawers are filled with kitchen towels, cooking utensils and lids. The mundane nature of it bothers me.

I check the spices but find nothing, no hidden USBs, no other devices. Ula's footsteps are loud and fast. She's halfway down the stairs before I manage to pour some water in a glass, taking a sip as I walk back to the living room.

Could she have heard me snooping around? Surely not with all the noise she was making.

'Don't open the closet,' she says, 'or you'll get buried in my junk.'

'I won't even unpack,' I say.

As she glances across the room, her gaze lingers on the bar area that separates the living room from the kitchen. The vein in my neck begins to throb. Has she noticed that I moved the spices?

'Will you stay for dinner or do you have plans?'

'I really don't want to impose.'

I'd love nothing more than to eat Ula's food and not just because my signature dish is a posh cheese sandwich. Ever since she moved out, her creamy curry has featured frequently in my dreams.

'Oh, please,' she says and heads to the kitchen. 'It's no trouble at all.'

I sit at the bar and watch Ula assemble the cooking utensils and vegetables on the counter. She starts lining up the spices.

'If you don't feel like cooking, I could order something for us.'

Ula drops her chin and frowns at me.

'Please. When did I ever not feel like cooking? Besides, you wouldn't want to eat the things they deliver around here.'

She strips the onion of its peel in a few moves. 'To have the audacity to call that rubbish cuisine,' she adds.

'I do miss your cooking.'

'Is curry alright?' she asks. 'I won't make it too spicy.'

I press my lips together and think of the massive pot of curry she used to make for us. It was so creamy it cuddled your tongue. I'd fight others over the leftovers.

'Can I help?' I ask.

Ula takes a bottle of wine out of the fridge. 'Open this, will you?'

She tosses a corkscrew onto the counter. I uncork the bottle and pour two glasses. Meanwhile, Ula is peeling the carrots with long and elegant strokes.

'Whom are you interviewing? Anyone famous?'

'Some CEO guy who knows about patents.'

'You're still with the same newspaper?' she asks. 'The one that published your corporate guilt article?'

My cheeks flush. 'Still there, yes.'

'I thought it was pretty good.'

I take a long sip. 'My editor likes this corporate stuff.'

'Didn't you win an award?'

'I was nominated,' I say, 'but I didn't get it.'

Ula takes another sip. 'A matter of time, I'm sure.'

While I appreciate Ula's flattery, I'm also a bit worried. It wasn't supposed to be me talking about work, but the other way around.

'I always thought you'd stick with music stuff,' she says, 'or end up writing mysteries or something. With all those Agatha Christie books you were hoarding.'

'Actually, I *am* writing a book.'

'A journalist *and* a novelist.'

'It's not a novel,' I say. 'More like a book-length article.'

'Go on.'

'I'm doing research on intellectual property in companies. Protection, theft, that kind of stuff.'

I avoid looking into her eyes for fear of giving something away. She wouldn't remember the time when I asked her to lend me a USB and she said she didn't have any. Later, I borrowed one from her drawer. It contained an impressive number of documents, none of which were publicly available.

'Copyright?' she asks.

'Patents. Ways companies protect their secrets and what happens when they get stolen.'

'And?'

'If they can prove it, good for them. If they can't, though, the best they can do is spy back. It's usually their competition anyway.'

Ula blinks, then drains her wine. 'Another one?' Without waiting for an answer, she tops up our glasses. 'The curry shouldn't take too long,' she says. 'Still no peanuts, right?'

'Unless you want to kill me,' I say.

She laughs.

'Let's leave that for tomorrow, when you wake me up at five a.m.'

When Ula begins to slice the vegetables, her face gains the sharp sort of focus I know so well. I've learned not to disturb her. This time, however, I'm tempted to see if I can tease out the answers I came for.

I don't need to fake curiosity. Ever since Ula went off social media, she ghosted out on all old friends. Every so often, I send her a message. Her answers are quick and brief without leaving much space for follow-up. If her name hadn't popped up in a confidential database, I'd probably have given up.

'What about you?' I ask. 'Happy with that tech firm? Sorry, I forgot their name.'

'Nah,' she says. 'I went freelance a while back.'

'You're in IT, though?'

'What can I say?' she winks at me. 'I'm a one-trick pony.'

As she slices the onion, her hands create a dancing movement, like a wave. She's so fast her eyes don't get the chance to water.

I lick my lips. 'I always figured you'd be a chef,' I say.

She laughs.

'Mixing pleasure and business is like pouring oil onto fire,' she says.

'I suppose fixing people's computers is somewhat less complicated,' I say.

'I don't actually fix stuff,' Ula says. 'I just check their system safety and tell them to sort out their mess.'

'Does it work?'

'It freaks them out enough for them to start to throw cash at me to tell them how to fix it.'

She squirts some oil into a pan.

'Don't they have back-up?'

'It's not about back-up,' she says and turns on the heat. 'I could tell you more, but then I'd have to charge.'

She tosses the onions into the pan and stirs them with a wooden spoon.

'I'll need to stay with this for a bit so it doesn't burn,' she says. 'If you want to freshen up, this would be a good time.'

I'm reluctant to lose precious time on personal hygiene, especially now that we're on topic, so I take a sip of wine.

'The towels are in the cabinet. If you need anything else, give me a shout.'

Ula rubs the spices between her palms and lets them drop into the sizzling pot. She's so completely absorbed, I know I won't manage to distract her.

'I do need a shower,' I say and go upstairs. If nothing else, I have some time to look for evidence.

The guest room is cosy, hardly bigger than the queen-sized bed. Above the bed hangs an elegant ink drawing of some bamboo. I don't know much about Asian art, but it appears to be genuine, nothing like the Ikea prints in my studio. I don't bother opening the closet. If there is anything worth hiding, Ula has probably hidden it somewhere else.

I grab a fresh outfit and head to the bathroom. The space is oddly familiar. I need a few moments to realise why. It resembles a bathroom in an office or a hotel, a bathroom for other people.

White and blue towels are folded on the shelf. There's a fresh bar of soap by the sink and a small bottle of vanilla-scented incense with wooden stalks sticking out. When we still shared a flat, Ula had a habit of buying quirky bargains at the flea market and filling all empty space with Aladdin-style lamps, colourful jewellery boxes and floral china. Sure, people's behaviour can change, but what about their personality?

After a quick shower, I leave the water running to cover the noise of my search. I examine the small cabinet above the sink. A few painkillers and contact lens liquid. Does Ula wear glasses? I can't remember seeing her with them. It could also be just one of those extra items people keep for others.

On my way back, I pass another door, supposedly Ula's bedroom. I pull the doorknob. It's locked. Did she lock it after tidying the guest room?

When I return downstairs, everything smells of butter and onion.

'Found what you needed?' Ula asks.

My chest tightens. 'More than that,' I say. 'I'm jealous of your house.'

Ula covers the pot. The rumble dies out. She moves to the bar where a few carrot sticks are dished up in a cream mug, along with a plate of hummus.

'When did you have time to make this?' I ask.

'Yesterday.'

We scoop up some hummus with a carrot stick and eat it. It's smooth and luxurious. I want to tell her how amazing it is, but instead I take another carrot stick and shovel the hummus into my mouth.

'Wow,' I say. 'This beats anything I ever bought in a store.'

'They don't add enough tahini and lemon juice,' Ula says.

'Is that the secret?'

'That and baking soda. I add some when I soak the chickpeas. It makes them softer.'

'How did you come up with that?'

'I learned it in a workshop.'

'Which one? I might take it.'

'You'd have to go to the Middle East.'

I wait to see if she'll elaborate. She doesn't.

'Not exactly your typical holiday destination,' I say.

'It was for work.'

I sense a hint of annoyance in her voice, but I've come too far to give up.

'Where else have you been?'

'No tropical islands, if that's what you think.'

She hands me a fresh glass of wine. 'Things I get to see are limited to airports and meeting rooms.'

'I'd love to travel more,' I say in an attempt to soften the atmosphere.

Her jaw tightens. She breaks a carrot stick in half. I get a pang of guilt for pressing so hard.

'Tell me more about your patent stuff,' she says. 'How does it work?'

'Pretty much like normal espionage,' I say, 'but between companies. They find ways to steal each other's secrets. Sometimes they hire other people to do it. You know, like Hans.'

Ula cocks an eyebrow.

'The exchange student in your study group?'

'What study group?'

'Math, I think. Not sure. He studied engineering.'

Ula chews on the carrots. Her face gives nothing away.

'Oh, yes. Hans the square-face. He was quite smart.'

'The best in his class. He landed some fancy job at a big shot carmaker.'

'I don't see your point,' she says.

'You didn't stay in touch?'

Ula looks at me as though I've said something outrageous.

'Why would I?'

I decide not to mention the files on Ula's USB, a neat collection of internal documents about IT systems of all the major carmakers.

'Well, he got quite high up the ladder before he vanished. Thought you might have heard anything.'

Ula perks up.

'Anyway, I forgot all about it until I read that a German carmaker launched a new type of engine. Something to do with noise reduction and sustainability – all gibberish to me. Seems the exact same engine was being developed in Hans's old company, but the plans disappeared, roughly at the same time as Hans.'

'He stole them?'

'I suppose so but they couldn't prove it.'

Ula doesn't appear surprised to hear the story.

'Why risk his career?' she asks.

'He probably got paid to study here. Stayed long enough to get what he needed, then took it back home.'

'Is that how it works?'

My gut twists. Ula knows exactly how it works. If I hadn't accidentally copied all those files from Ula's USB, I wouldn't have known they were classified trade secrets. There was no way she could get her hands on them by accident. She had to be the one helping Hans. How else could she have gotten the money to buy the apartment?

We take a long sip of wine.

'It's not uncommon for spies to have high-flying jobs,' I say. 'You know, managers, heads of department.'

Or consultants. I don't say that, of course.

The pots rattle. Reluctantly, Ula stirs the contents, but her focus is gone. 'You still smoke?' she asks.

'Sometimes.'

'I'm dying for a cigarette. Let's have one in the garden.'

'I'll get my bag.'

I don't feel like smoking, but she might open up, as usual, after a glass of wine. As I fetch my bag from the guest room, I spot a small door at the end of the corridor, the size of a cabinet. I lean over the banister to check on Ula. The scraping of pots convinces me she's still busy, so I pull the door handle. The door opens.

At first glimpse, it's a storage space like any other. A vacuum cleaner, a mop, a few dirty rugs and a cardboard box with cleaning products. Have my instincts let me down? I'm about to leave when I notice a shimmer at the bottom of the box.

The floorboards creak as I move the box. There are a few items that look like they've been dropped there. A USB flash recorder, similar to the one I saw online when searching for spyware. Why would Ula need to hide that she's recording someone's voice? Next to it is a small round box that looks like a speaker but contains a hidden camera. Another item I discovered thanks to my internet search. Ula must have tossed them in there in a hurry.

A loud noise comes from downstairs and I scuttle out of the room.

'Everything alright up there?' Ula shouts.

I tug at the bag strap on my shoulder. 'Yup! Just couldn't find my lighter.'

She barely looks at me when I come down. We go into the garden. The sky is the colour of dark plum jam. I light her cigarette. Despite the cosy looking wooden bench, we stand. Ula puffs out a few perfect rings of smoke.

'You've always wanted to be a journo, haven't you?' she says. 'I remember you scribbling, taking notes.'

I dig my heels into the grass.

'Not sure if I'd say always, but the work is alright. What about you? I guess you haven't always wanted to be a consultant.'

'It pays well.'

'That's where I went wrong,' I say.

Ula tilts back her head. 'Aren't you worried you'll piss people off? With stuff you write?'

'Too late for that.'

'I mean the wrong people.'

'People with something to hide, you mean?'

'People obsessed with their privacy.'

Beads of sweat gather in the small of my back.

'That would mean I'm getting lucky,' I say.

Ula smiles, but her eyes remain cold.

'How so?' she asks.

'If I piss someone off, it's usually for a good reason.'

She turns towards a distant point on the horizon and lets the smoke crawl out of her mouth. 'How do you find them?' she asks. 'I mean, when they don't want to be found.'

'I have my sources – a hacker, two retired spies.'

She gives me a perfunctory smile and rolls the cigarette between her fingers. The burning orange dot glows one more time, then she stubs it out.

'Another one?' I offer.

'I don't want the curry to burn,' she says.

'Mind if I do?'

'Go ahead.'

I light another cigarette as if to demonstrate intent. When Ula leaves, I take out my phone and turn on the app that tracks hidden cameras. It's a free version of bug finder but does the trick. The cursor points at the huge flowerpot by the door. The camera is the same colour as the clay pot and points at the entrance door. According to my research, this could be the type of camera with a facial recognition technology.

Upstairs, Ula is washing her hands in her in-built bathroom. She'll be in a hurry to finish dinner. I put out the cigarette, go back inside and dump my bag on the sofa. When Ula heads back down, I head up the stairs.

'Going to wash my hands,' I say.

'Curry needs another minute,' she says, 'but we can set the table.'

I leave the tap running as I sneak into Ula's bedroom. The door is closed but not locked, just as I suspected. The blinds are down. With my app, I scan for cameras. There are none. When my eyes adjust, I make out three rectangular shapes: a bed, a bedside cabinet and a closet. I open the closet. An array of dark suits and white blouses. Shoes are lined up at the bottom, shoeboxes stacked in the back.

The top shoebox contains black, expensive-looking stilettos. The ones underneath are red. The bottom shoebox is full of discs labelled with numbers. So that's where Ula keeps her finds, the stuff she steals from companies while she gives them advice on IT security. Sleek.

I take one of the CDs but it slips from my hands and falls onto the floor. I crawl in the dark until I find it and put it back. Blood gushes between my ears as I leave the room. I half expect to find Ula standing in the corridor, but it's empty. I close the tap in the bathroom and flush the toilet one more time.

Below, the table is set with two napkins folded into a fan. Ula is carrying the curry pot.

'Good that I'm not on a diet,' I say.

'Diets are stupid anyway,' she says.

I don't know why I smile, but tension ripples inside my gut. I've betrayed Ula and put our friendship on the line, but one could argue she's done the same a long time ago. Or does she think she's protecting her friends by keeping distance from them?

'I know I've said it before,' I say, 'but you're a damned fine cook.'

The pot thuds as she puts it on the table. She opens the lid and steam rises from it like a blurry curtain.

There's a shift in the air, as if the words have become electrified, charged. Could she have had motion and temperature-recording sensors somewhere in the room? I didn't think of that before.

'Would you mind bringing the rice?' she asks.

'Sure.'

I head to the kitchen. As I carry the rice to the table, Ula is plating the curry. She plucks a few coriander leaves from a small pot on the table and places them on top of her plate.

'None for you, I suppose,' she says.

'Nope, still hate it,' I say.

'Apparently, it's the genes,' she says, without raising her gaze.

I top up our wine glasses.

'Here's to old friends,' I say, 'and great cooks.'

I take tiny bites so as not to burn my tongue. Each spoonful is an eruption of flavour in my mouth. It's spicy, though, enough to bring tears to my eyes.

'It's absolutely delicious,' I say, 'but I can't handle my spice.'

Ula smiles.

'You're getting old,' she says. 'I used less than half of my usual chilis.'

'That won't stop me from eating it,' I say.

'That's why you're here,' she says, smiling. 'Admit it.'

Maybe it's the wine-induced confidence or my natural inclination to keep digging that makes me push further.

'I did want to ask you something.'

'Ask away.'

'It's about my book. One of my sources got access to a database. A confidential one.'

'The hacker?'

'It was a list of suspects. People listed as potential spies.'

She holds her fork, but she doesn't take more food.

'You want me to track down these people?' she asks. 'You know I can't do that. It's very illegal.'

'Your name was there.'

'You're kidding, right?'

'Your nickname, actually. The one you used back then.'

She purses her lips.

'What, Bamb1? I haven't used that since the nineties.'

Her shoulders stiffen and her knuckles lose colour. We chew in silence.

'Sarah,' she says, 'just what exactly are you implying?'

She doesn't look up.

'I'm not implying anything. Just sharing what I know.'

'I thought journos were supposed to know the difference between a hint and a proof.'

The pit of my stomach starts to tingle. Out of all the things I want to say to Ula, some are the ones I should say, like the fact that I could link her nickname to at least one IP address she owned.

'I am getting proof,' I say, 'but I'm also drafting the book.'

'Sounds more like you're drafting a gossip column.'

'I never skip my research. Doesn't mean I have to sit and wait.'

'Maybe you should be writing a thriller instead.'

When I look up, Ula's wearing a sly smile. My neck tightens. Normally, I'd shrug such remarks off, make a joke, but this time I can't. If I give Ula the proof, she's going to clam up. She might even kick me out. Then what?

What bothers me, though, is her mocking and deceit. A part of me knows I need to pull back. This other part needs to push, to shake Ula's lies and point a flashlight right at them.

'I'll start with an article,' I say. 'My editor thinks it could shake things up, get people to talk.'

'What article?'

'A teaser while I do the research. To keep things warm and interesting.'

'And you won't need evidence to write this article?'

'Not if it's broad strokes and generic stuff.'

'How generic?'

'I don't have to name names. I could give people nicknames. Say Bamb1, female, middle-aged, works in IT security.'

Her fork slips and hits the porcelain plate.

'I'm not middle-aged,' Ula says. 'Why do you want to get me in trouble?'

'If I poke in the right direction, maybe people will start talking.'

My shirt feels tight around my chest.

'What if you poke too hard?'

'What's too hard?'

'Someone might grab the other end of the stick.'

'So? I'd get a new source.'

'It wouldn't just be a source, would it? They'd want to keep you close by all means possible.'

I scoop the last bits of curry from my plate.

'It'd still be a source,' I say.

'Not if you have to hold on to that stick,' she says.

I shrug.

Ula brings a jug of water and pours two glasses.

'Is it true that Elena got divorced?' she asks. 'I hear her fishmonger business is blooming, though.'

I exhale loudly and drain my water. For the next half an hour, we exchange gossip about our former classmates. I'm surprised how well-informed she is. Afterwards, we clear the table and load the dishwasher.

'Time to flex that extra stomach,' Ula says.

I blow a raspberry. After two helpings of curry, I hardly have enough space to breathe.

'I'm done, babe.'

Ula hands me two plates.

'You can't skip dessert,' she says and opens the fridge. 'It's my new favourite cake.'

On the plate is a small, dark cake topped with sliced oranges.

'Chocolate?' I ask.

'It's based on some famous velvet cake recipe but I improvised. You have to try it.'

'Alright,' I say. 'A small piece.'

'Why don't you cut it?' she asks. 'I'll make some coffee. Still black? No sugar?'

'Make it double.'

I cut a thin slice for me and a bigger one for Ula, then eat the crumbs from the plate. The caramel flavour wraps around my tongue like silk.

I finish my piece in a few bites. Ula eats slowly and deliberates each bite, as if she's trying to improve the recipe in her head. I consider cutting another small piece when I unexpectedly sneeze.

'Bless you.'

I blow my nose a few times. It doesn't stop running and there's a persistent tickling at the back of my throat, too.

'Have more water,' Ula says and pours it into my glass.

As I drink it, I become aware of an itch on my face, the raw kind, that makes me want to plough over my skin with a fork. Then it hits me.

'Peanuts,' I say. 'Where are they?'

Ula glances at her wristwatch.

'There are no peanuts in the cake, Sarah.'

I start to cough.

'In the curry, then.'

'It's not peanuts,' she says with the cold composure of someone explaining statistics. 'Just some peanut butter.'

The air gets broiling hot. I struggle to breathe. My tongue is growing bigger. My throat is like a fire burning down a ravine. Soon, my face will swell. I won't see properly. Then, I'll start to choke.

I leap to the sofa, grab my bag and turn it over. The contents scatter on the floor. I scan over them. There's the notepad, a half-dozen pens, my lipstick and cigarettes, some loose change. My heart is thundering like crazy.

'You looking for this?' Ula asks, holding my EpiPen between her fingers.

I try to snatch it, but the horizon distorts into a myriad of pulsing dots. I clutch my throat and stumble to the ground.

Ula checks her wristwatch.

'You've got about a minute, maybe two, before you pass out,' she says. 'Shall I get to it?'

I try to speak but all that comes out of my mouth is a gurgle. I nod violently.

'To get the work done, you'll need to learn when to stop,' she says.

My mouth is open, something is blocking the air.

'Luckily, I'm a good teacher. And journos make efficient spies.'

The world shrinks into a thin strip of light. Beneath me, the ground shakes. Or maybe I'm shaking.

I thump onto the floor.

'Congratulations on your new job,' Ula says and kneels next to me.

The last thing I feel, before I dip into darkness, is a jab of pain as Ula stabs the EpiPen into my leg.

DASH FRIEND

Her husband grew up with exclamation marks. She only discovered this when they visited his family. As they arrived, his mother threw her hands into the air.

'You should have called!' she said.

'We didn't want you to worry, Mum.'

What his father lacked in height, he made up for in roar.

'Well, don't just stand there!' he said. 'Come in, come in!'

He patted them on the shoulder and carried the suitcases inside. From the moment they sat down, his mother started to lay out food on the table.

'Eat, eat!' she said.

'We're not that hungry,' her husband said.

'You have to try my courgette strudel!'

As they were stuffing their faces with strudel and biscuits, she observed exclamation marks popping in and out of the conversation.

Must be the excitement.

Their enthusiasm didn't die out till they retired to their rooms. She wanted to hear her husband's opinion on the matter, but he fell asleep before she'd finished brushing her teeth. Her thoughts swirled to the rhythm of his snore. She examined all the blotches on the wall and counted the irregularities on the floral wallpaper, then decided to do some work. She was editing an article when exclamation marks started to drop on the other side of the wall.

Quietly, she climbed out of bed and pressed her ear against the wallpaper. Staccato words rapped like the heavy drops of a summer storm, at times at low pitch, at times at a higher one. The words were muffled, so she wasn't sure what her in-laws were saying, but the tone was as dark and bitter as the coffee at breakfast.

For the rest of their visit, she acted as if nothing had happened and refrained from unpacking her suitcase to speed up the departure. They bid farewell with an abundance of noise. She and her husband hardly spoke on their way home. Once they arrived, her husband dropped the bags on the floor and flopped into his armchair.

'It's so nice and quiet,' he said, putting his feet up.

Their eyes met and they burst into laughter.

'Are they always like this?' she asked.

'Not always,' he said. 'It's much worse when my uncle is there. He shouts at the sky in case it rains.'

They laughed till their eyes brimmed with tears and their lungs whistled. Their shaking bellies confirmed that such silly habits had no place in their home. They had no need for exclamation marks, certainly not the kind one couldn't laugh about.

So reassured was she by their agreement, that she let the first one slip by unremarked. Was it even an exclamation mark or mere jest? She wouldn't want to ruin a perfectly good joke.

The second one nearly slipped by under the radar. They were unpacking a set of beautiful porcelain plates, a gift from his parents, when one of them fell.

Carefully, she examined the delicate bluebird drawings and spotted a thin crack, no thicker than an eyelash.

'God damn it!' her husband said.

'We can still use it.'

'Are you sure?'

'Of course.'

He kissed her on the forehead.

'It's alright,' she said to no one in particular. He smiled and kissed her again, this time full on her lips.

The third exclamation mark leapt out of nowhere as they were leaving for dinner with his boss.

'I told you about the fixed menu!' he said.

'Not what's on it.'

'We can't cancel!'

'We don't have to.'

'You can't eat the clam soup. It'll make you sick!'

'I'll pretend I'm eating.'

'They'll think you hate it!'

'It'll be alright.'

After that night, she found more exclamation marks than she cared to admit. Where had they been hiding? Every time she checked, there were more, shamelessly parading around with their messages. They took their courtesies hostage. The morning hellos, she didn't mind. Her consciousness would still be rattled from waking up and she needed time before she could fully inhabit herself. The evening ones bothered her, though. They made words sound harsher, more permanent.

'I'm off to bed!'

'Don't wait up!'

By the time she considered raising this with her husband, the exclamation marks had infested entire conversations.

'Have you been to the store?!'

'Not yet!'

'Get mustard. Not the cheap one like last time!'

How was she to bring this up? They never discussed punctuation as such, certainly not as a serious matter. He might shrug it off as an editor's quirk or accuse her of blowing things out of proportion. Besides, hadn't they banned the offending marks from their house? Hadn't they agreed so in laughter?

The only way she could address this was to wrap it up as a

joke. She thought of a dozen, but none seemed quite right. The punchline had to be light enough not to cause offence but carry enough substance to make the point.

That evening, she prepared her husband's favourite dish, spaghetti carbonara with extra sauce. He wiped the plate clean and grunted with pleasure. By the time she'd finished washing the dishes, her husband was sitting in his armchair with a newspaper folded in his lap.

Her heart kicked.

'Aren't things getting a bit too quiet?'

He tipped his head to one side.

'What do you mean?'

She drew in a long breath and yelled, 'We hardly ever shout anymore!'

Her husband's eyes narrowed, the way they did when she teased him about having an affair with his car. He unfolded the newspaper and started to read.

'I'm sorry,' she said. 'It was a bad joke.'

He hid his face behind the printed page and said nothing.

The exclamation marks popped up less often after that. She learned to read the signs: a slight change in the air, a drop in the temperature, a loud kind of silence that hung around the corners. Soon afterwards, her husband's nostrils would flare and his ears would close to everything except his thoughts.

At night, she wondered about the exclamation marks. Was there a way to make them disappear? To make sure they would no longer pester her? Even with her eyes closed, she saw them, the stern creatures marching around with no shame or respect for other punctuation.

She flipped one upside down and spun it, like a clock's hands. Doing this soothed her. The more she thought about it, the clearer it became that she saw two separate creatures. One was small and round, like a full stop, while the other one was long and thin, like a dash.

Aren't you two an interesting pair? A full stop and its dash friend.

The idea delighted her. All she had to do was translate the offending marks into more agreeable punctuation.

Next time her husband's nostrils quivered, she reached for her new tools.

'When are we meeting the Walkers again?' she asked.

Electric silence buzzed in her ears.

'Did you really forget?! We told them we wouldn't!'

What an elegant dash.

'Oh, sorry. Must have slipped my mind.'

'Why don't you write these things down?!'

Translating drained so much energy that she struggled to keep up. Could she learn not to see the exclamation marks? With gritted teeth, she started to wipe them out. First the full stop, then the elegant dash friend. The latter sometimes appeared thin and sharp, other times wider and triangular. She didn't like to look at it for too long. No matter how she flipped it, one of its sharp edges always seemed to be pointing directly at her.

Occasionally, the elegant dash stung her. She wouldn't complain, though.

It's only a scratch.

She considered that while spooning more cereal into her mouth. Something crunched between her teeth. She spat the food into a napkin.

'What's the matter?' her husband asked.

As she ran her tongue over her teeth, she discovered a dent.

'Looks like my tooth chipped.'

'Go to the dentist.'

'It doesn't hurt.'

'Not yet, but once it does, you won't shut up about it.'

'I'm sure it's nothing.'

'For God's sake, call him!'

Her dentist, an old gentleman with a distinguished beard and expensive glasses, let out many 'hmms' and 'ohhs', as he restored the chipped tooth.

'If I were you,' he said, 'I'd get a mouthguard.'

She couldn't speak with her mouth open, so she made gargling sounds as she rinsed her mouth. Still, the dentist understood.

'It's a piece of silicon that will help you stop grinding your teeth,' he said.

'I don't grind my teeth.'

'It's quite common,' the dentist said in his velvety voice. 'Many people do it in their sleep.'

'In my sleep? Impossible!'

The dentist's eyes widened.

'Nothing to be ashamed of,' he said and rearranged the drills. 'I use one myself.'

'Well, I won't!'

His hand jerked as if he'd touched a live wire. At once, she regretted using the full stop with the elegant dash. She apologised profusely, not so much with words as with the abundance of pleasantries reserved for good friends. On her way home, her mind buzzed and fuelled her steps with blind haste and ineptitude.

When had the exclamation marks sneaked into her sentences? How come she hadn't noticed? Could she un-learn it? Was there an antidote to the invasive duo? She would gladly abandon punctuation entirely, if it meant she'd never have to see another offensive mark.

That evening, her husband asked for spaghetti carbonara but they'd run out of bacon, so she improvised with tuna.

'How was the dentist?' he asked.

'He says I need a mouthguard.'

'A what?!'

He put down his fork.

'Some plastic to put between my teeth.'

He shook his head.

'What a load of crap! You didn't agree, did you?!'

'Of course not!'

'No need to shout!'

'I'm not shouting!'

The next morning, the plates were still on the table, smudged with leftover sauce. The dried-out chunks of tuna reminded her of the things TV doctors cut out of their patients.

As she scraped it off the plates, a few stubborn pieces stuck to the cracked part of the porcelain. Reluctant to touch it, she whacked the plate against the bin, harder than intended.

Oh no!

The fracture had deepened and now ran across the whole plate. Eventually, the tiny pieces would chip, like her tooth, and split the plate in half. Tossing the dish away would save her the trouble of having it fall apart in her hands, possibly while loaded with a steaming meal.

He won't like that.

Would he notice, though? He never washed the dishes, and he didn't count them, either. She poked the rubbish aside and placed the cracked plate at the bottom. Later on, she'd take the rubbish out. No one would ever find out what had happened.

As she was getting dressed, she heard a weird clank coming from the kitchen. The air stirred. A whiff of something rotten entered the living room.

'Don't bother with the rubbish!' she said. 'I'll take it out.'

The silence that followed rang in her ears. When she entered the kitchen, her husband stood in the middle of the room holding up the cracked plate, still shiny with grease.

'You did this?!'

'I'm sorry. I didn't mean to, but I... I...'

With pursed lips, he examined the evidence against the light.

'It's not even broken!'

The dish began slipping from his grip until the porcelain smashed against the tiled floor.

She blinked at the shards of porcelain, then at her husband. With his flushed cheeks and his hand still up, he looked like a misplaced statue. She didn't want to laugh, swear to God she didn't, but her mouth stretched into a grin.

'You think this is funny?!'

The vein on her husband's neck pulsed like a toad's mouth. She should have apologised, said something to calm him down, but before she could, some other words came out.

'It's hilarious!' she heard herself say.

More words shot out, as if in a hurry to escape. None were the words she'd normally use, yet she found them strangely fitting. Her husband's cheeks turned crimson.

'What did you call me?!'

This was the time to retreat, to take everything back. She found, though, that she couldn't.

'In the end, it was you who broke it!'

Ripples of laughter shook her like a rattle. She tried to explain why she'd thrown the damned plate away, but her voice sounded like a broken whistle, which made her crack up more.

'Stop laughing!!!'

His eyes were narrow, like a snake's.

'I caaaaaan't!!!'

The harder she tried to contain her laughter, the stronger the thunder between her ears. The tears turned the world into a wash of colours. Her husband's face changed but she couldn't say how. Was he laughing or was the light playing tricks on her?

Her roar mushroomed until it devoured all other sounds and thoughts. It occurred to her that it might devour her, too, if she dared to stop laughing.

As she blinked away the tears, she caught a glimpse of her husband picking something up from the floor. Was he cleaning up? The sheer thought that such a miracle could occur made her howl.

She could no longer stand, so she leaned forwards, lost her balance and fell onto the floor, laughing.

What she saw next made little sense: the triangular dash, shaped like a piece of the broken plate. Was it pointing at her? What she was sure of was that it looked like a dagger. And it was coming closer and closer.

GARDENER'S SENSE

I like to get my hands dirty when the day is still fresh and untainted. With a hot cuppa in my hands, I snuggle into my garden chair and watch my lovelies rouse from their sleep. The dew glimmers on their leaves like night tears, drying before morning.

Once the horizon turns golden and sunlight licks the darkness away, the first hikers are bound to come trotting out of the forest. It doesn't take long for someone to stop by to say hi or to chat. The latter, I've learned, is often pretence for something else, something they want like a glass of water, a hint where to pick mushrooms or a really quick loo stop.

Jack loved talking to strangers. He'd wave at them and offer them a glass of his elderflower soda or a sandwich, if they seemed hungry. He knew how hungry the forest could make you. He listened to people's stories, nodded as they chattered along, always agreeable, always supportive. I began to suspect that people returned just for the chat. What else is there to do in a small town like ours?

I miss those days.

The best I manage on my own is being polite.

'How d'you do? Yes, the weather's been lovely. You're right, things might always change.'

I don't have Jack's wordiness or his charm, but that doesn't mean I don't know how to read people's faces. I notice their eyes sliding from side to side, how they start to crumple the hems on their sleeves, how they avoid looking at me, when they talk about the way things used to be. No one wants to say it, no one cares to spell it out, but I know what they think. I'm not the only one who misses him.

People and plants aren't that different. Give them enough attention, treat them with respect, and they'll reward you with love and loyalty. Disregard their needs or cross their limits, and you might discover a whole different side to them.

Once a problem is in plain sight, everyone can spot it. What takes knowledge and skill is detecting the early signs, understanding what's going to happen. A gardener's sense is as much a gift as a burden.

Take the hydrangea, for example. A year ago, she was on the verge of collapse, all because of the orchid convention. I had this strange feeling before I left, as though something wasn't quite right. Her leaves were sagging a bit, as if from the heat, but I couldn't be sure. When I tried to check, Jack insisted there wasn't enough time because I'd miss my train. He'd take care of it, he said, promised he'd keep an eye and take good care of my lovelies.

I couldn't relax, though, not when there was a chance that the whiteflies had come back. They are persistent little buggers, hard to spot and even harder to get rid of. They suck out your plant's juices and infest the leaves with their pale eggs. You can't spot them, unless you know what you're looking for. By the time you notice something is wrong, it's too late.

Whiteflies are as sneaky as they are greedy. They're especially fond of my peppers and tomatoes, but when given a chance, they'll gladly devour anything, even flowers. I had to part with my calendula and camomile, but I sure as hell wasn't going bid farewell to my hydrangea. Not when it was my wedding present to Jack. It took me years to cultivate the right shade of blue, the exact colour of Jack's eyes.

That's why you mustn't lose time when you're fighting against whiteflies. If you take too long to think, they'll destroy everything you care for.

In your first plan of attack, you need to isolate the plant, hose it down and kill any bugs that don't fall off. You must leave no survivors. These little vampires will suck out all the plant's juices till you have nothing left. Once you've taken care of this, you'll need to protect your lovelies. I prefer to use my own remedies because they're kind to the plants, yet efficient with the pests. To begin with, you can spray your plants with a mild mix of soapy water.

A proper infestation calls for stronger medicine. You can't go wrong with a mix of water, coconut soap and kerosene. Wait till sundown, then spray it over your lovelies. After that, keep a close watch and rely on the gardener's sense.

Caring for plants must be similar to taking care of children. You take care for their needs and do what you can to protect them. At least plants don't move out and leave, like children do. My lovelies have always been there for me. It's only fair that I return the favour.

I caress the hydrangea's luscious white petals, kiss them softly and give the soil a generous splash of water.

'You look cheerful today,' I say.

It's hard to believe that the same petals were once drooping with utter sadness. If I hadn't returned home early, if the orchid convention hadn't been cut short, who knows what would have happened.

I expected to find Jack in the garden but he wasn't home. He enjoyed going to the forest as often as he could but I didn't think he'd forget about his promise. I couldn't blame him, though. His eyes were accustomed to appreciating beauty. He'd never spot something as small and vicious as a whitefly. Was I wrong to expect he'd care about my lovelies as I do? Perhaps. I certainly didn't expect to have to wait for him till the small hours of the morning.

He was surprised to find me home, startled even, but not nearly as much as I was when he leaned in for a kiss. The floral fragrance on Jack's neck hadn't come from a flower. No perfume can replicate the gentle, fragile scent of jasmine. Besides, jasmine doesn't grow where we live.

We held each other's gaze, Jack and I, and let our eyes speak in silence. Jack was the first one to turn away. Naive as I was, I expected him to apologise, to beg for forgiveness. He didn't, though. What he said was not what I wanted to hear. Afterwards, we had no more need for words. A gardener's sense tells you when to fight, but also when it's time to give up.

I couldn't desert my lovelies, though. They needed me. Nursing them back to health kept me busy. A busy mind has no time to dwell. I had to protect my lovelies, clean them up and feed them with fresh nutrients. Once the cool winds started to blow, snow covered the soil and everything grew quiet. The tree branches were coated with ice, like ballerinas in diamond dresses. I embraced the quiet and took my chance to retreat. It wasn't too long before the sun teased the world back to life.

A year later, my hydrangea thanked me with delightful white flowers. Hydrangeas can surprise you like that. A slight change in soil acidity can turn their blossoms pink, white or purple. It's not only people who get to have a fresh start. I learned so much from my lovelies about life, change and resilience.

As soon as I catch a whiff of a sweet fragrance, I pause. Gemma's perfume announces her presence before she appears on the mud path.

'Ange! A lovely day, isn't it?'

She leans onto the wooden gates of my garden. Her smile is almost as wide as her hips.

'Going back already?' I ask.

'I have to,' she says. 'I've got too much work.'

Her shoes and hiking poles are caked in mud which, incidentally, is the same colour as her eyes.

'Busy times at the office?' I pluck a few weeds from under my rosebush.

'You can say that again.' She wipes the sweat away with her sleeve. 'The whole place is going crazy over the summer sales. What about you? Your flower shop doing alright?'

'I'm not complaining.'

'You never do, Ange. Doesn't mean you couldn't.'

She scans the garden, as if assessing the state of my lovelies. Good old Gemma, always in search of a fresh piece of gossip.

'No news, then?' she asks.

Slowly, I straighten up. 'About Jack, you mean?'

Our eyes meet for a short moment. She looks away.

'No, nothing.'

'Strange that he took off like that,' she says, 'without a word.'

'Not a single note left in the house.'

Her pudgy eyes narrow.

'What did you hear?' I ask.

She stabs a hiking pole into the ground. 'I don't believe rumours. You know that.'

I prune a few discoloured leaves from the rosebush.

'That doesn't stop them from spreading, does it?'

Gemma opens the wooden fence and enters the garden. The hiking poles dangle from her wrists like bracelets.

'So, you've heard them, too?' she asks.

'It's hardly news,' I say. 'The whole town thinks Jack left me for some young tart.'

'It's true, then?'

I shake the dew off the rosebush and snip a few stems. 'I don't know about that, but it's not impossible.'

Gemma taps the rosebuds, as if she's touching a hot plate.

'Don't worry,' I say. 'These don't have thorns.'

'Oh, I might try planting a couple of those,' she says, fondling one of the roses.

She won't, though. I know people like her. She likes the idea of roses in her backyard, but she's not willing to put in the hard work. That's why she never married.

'They're all the same, aren't they,' Gemma says. 'Men.'

'If by that you mean unreliable, you're onto something.' I cut off a few more rose stems and offer her the bouquet.

'Angela, you shouldn't.'

As she hugs me, I hold my breath so as not to inhale the sickly scent of her perfume.

'It's not so bad, you know,' she says. 'Being single.'

She sniffs at the bouquet once, twice, three times. The smell of jasmine on her skin is so overpowering, though, that I'd be surprised if she could smell anything else.

I walk over to my hydrangea. 'How are the twins?' I ask.

'Energetic as ever. It gets tiring.'

'I bet they'll break many hearts with those gorgeous blue eyes.'

The creases around her temples deepen. Then, she points at the hydrangea. 'A new addition?'

'Oh no,' I say. 'It's just the colour that's new.'

Gemma shuffles on her feet. 'How did you change it?'

'I added some sulphur, made the soil more acidic.'

'But why? Didn't you like blue?'

'It reminded me too much of Jack's eyes.'

She looks away and raises the rose bouquet. 'I'd better put these in a vase.'

'They'll keep for a few days.'

'Thanks, Ange. Gotta run now or I'll be late.'

'Take care, Gemma.'

She waves before grabbing her hiking poles and heading down the path. I wait. Once Gemma's outline is a small dot in the dirt, I put on my glasses. Examining the hydrangea for pests will take time. I'm not taking any more chances. Not after what we've been through.

To inspect the lower branches, I have to get down on my knees. The ground is still cold but I don't mind. The blossoms closest to the ground are the prettiest ones.

'My darling, you're absolutely gorgeous today.'

I cup a white blossom between my palms and inhale its luscious scent.

'White suits you much better than blue, too.'

My lips touch the ground as I suck in the musky smell of soil, the primal scent of creation and decay.

'Don't you think so, Jack?'

MOMENTS

Long shadows danced away from the headlights as Victoria and Oliver drove deeper into the forest. Victoria fought an impending headache. It didn't help that two radio channels were fighting for a single spot. She turned the dial until she got a clear sound, even if that meant she had to suffer classical music. If it was up to her, she'd turn it off altogether, but driving in silence and darkness was more than she could bear.

Oliver tried to avoid the bumps on the dirt road, but the further they drove, the more the road seemed to be imposing on the holes and bumps rather than the other way around.

'Watch out,' Victoria hissed.

'Sorry, love. My glasses fogged up,' Oliver said.

He didn't want to tell his wife he wasn't sure if they were on the right track. She had enough on her mind as it was.

'Put on the high beams.'

'I'm not sure it's a good idea,' Oliver said. 'On a small road like this, I mean.'

Victoria harrumphed. 'Call this a road…'

'You know how fast the locals drive when they think they're alone.'

Victoria frowned, but Oliver was too focused to notice.

'If by locals you mean bears and foxes, I think we're safe.'

Oliver smiled. 'It's a bit rural, I'll give you that.'

The vigorous squeaking of the wipers tried to outdo the clacking of the rain. Victoria tapped on the navigation system.

'We're lost, aren't we?' she said.

'We're not lost.'

'This road isn't even on the map.'

'Don't worry, love. I studied the map before we left.'

'As long as we aren't late,' Victoria said.

'How long will they hold our table for?'

Oliver focused on the road and missed the outraged expression on Victoria's face.

'They won't,' she said, still looking at him.

'Why not? They must know it takes some time to get there.'

Victoria pursed her lips. 'Did you even read the stuff I sent you?'

Though Oliver couldn't see his wife's face, he was well acquainted with the different grades of cold in her voice. He turned on the high beams. '*The Times*, you mean?' he asked.

'*The Times* and every freaking newspaper worth anything,' Victoria said. 'They have a waiting list for their waiting list. Do you think an exclusive restaurant like Moments is going to wait for us?'

'They won't have to, love.'

He didn't want to say more, for he'd only read the reservation details and that alone made for over forty pages of legal waffle. He'd struggled to get past page six. As far as Oliver was concerned, he'd be equally happy if they'd gone to their standard Italian place or something else less glamorous, but Victoria had been talking about Moments for months and he didn't want to appear ungrateful.

'I had to almost beg my client director to get the referral,' Victoria said. 'With all the sick days she's been taking for her son's tummy aches, she should be happy I don't fire her.'

Prokofiev's *The Love for Three Oranges* began to play on the radio.

'Why did they change it?' Oliver turned up the volume.

Victoria pursed her lips. It wasn't the first time her husband had continued a conversation in his head, expecting her to read his mind.

'Change what?' she asked, not trying to hide her irritation.

'The system. It wasn't like that when they first started, was it?'

'The referrals?' Victoria said. 'It's gotten into their head, that's why.'

'You don't reckon it has anything to do with a plan to keep Masterson out of the limelight?'

'Just how is that supposed to work, when everyone is writing about his new restaurant?'

'The restaurant, sure, but they're not writing about Richard Masterson, not since he sold off all of his other companies.'

Victoria frowned. If Richard Masterson wanted to get attention, he only had to stick his finger out the window and the media would come running. A wealthy widower, a cancer survivor and whatnot. Whatever he touched, the papers turned it to gold. If she was to race around in an expensive car and bring home men half her age, the papers would skin her alive, pick her clean like a bone. The papers weren't interested in her perfumes, only her failures.

Victoria flicked her crimson-painted nails. 'He's not exactly suffering, is he?'

'I meant the tragedy with his wife's death.'

Victoria let out a loud gust of air. Could Oliver possibly drive any slower? Sure, the conditions were far from ideal, but second gear?

'It's hardly a tragedy. Had she used a car, like normal people, not a helicopter, she'd be alive and well. If you think about it, it's his money that killed her.'

'You don't think her death hit him hard? There's hardly been any news about him since then.'

'Except in the yellow press.'

'I thought that was just gossip.' Oliver switched to first gear and drove around a large hole that took up most of the road.

'You give people too much credit,' Victoria said. 'Masterson is a vain man. He probably doesn't want to see his bald head in the papers.'

Their seatbelts yanked and pushed them against the car seats as the wheels got stuck in a patch of mud. The engine kept on revving.

'You'll sort this out, right?'

'Of course, love.'

Victoria stretched her feet as though to emphasise her new pair of high heels that matched her nail polish. The car lulled back and forth, splashing dirt all around.

'We'll look like we've come out of the jungle,' she said.

Oliver slowly added more power until the car drove back onto the solid road.

'There we go,' he said, as the engine began to purr.

A long line of trees with fairy lights wrapped around the trunks stretched ahead. Oliver parked and hurried to the other side of the car with an umbrella. Victoria retouched her lipstick and took Oliver's hand. The house ahead was a plain-looking building with a cream facade and brown window frames. Above the door was a dimly-lit sign that read 'Moments'.

The soft background music was overpowered by voluptuous aromas. At the entrance, a man in a black suit and white gloves stepped towards them.

'Welcome to Moments,' he said. 'I'm Ian, your host for the night.' His eyes drifted towards the tablet on the high oak table. 'You must be Mr and Mrs Evans.'

'That's right,' Victoria said. 'We've reserved for…'

'Eight o'clock?'

'We're not late, are we?' Oliver asked.

'Not at all,' said Ian and stretched out his hand. 'Let me take your coats. Is it your first time?'

'Take care,' Victoria pointed at the tiny puddle at Oliver's feet. 'You're dripping.'

Ian put the tablet away.

'Our reception is ready for you,' he said. 'We like to start by explaining our approach and philosophy.'

Victoria chuckled. 'Won't it ruin the surprise?'

Ian smiled. 'I'm afraid our policy doesn't allow us to serve food unless the guests have been acquainted with our way of working.'

Victoria bit her tongue. She hadn't eaten since breakfast and was in no mood to watch videos or listen to PowerPoint presentations. It was just a restaurant, for Christ's sake. These days, any business that finds its niche acts as if they've reinvented religion.

She drew in a breath, then gave Ian a toothy smile. 'Is this about the forty-two pages?' she asked. 'I did sign the agreement, as required.'

'Of course,' Ian said, 'but we only discuss details in person. I'm sure you understand.'

Victoria was about to protest when Oliver squeezed her hand. 'Maybe we should...'

Victoria shook off Oliver's hand and took a step forwards. She'd have none of this philosophy nonsense.

'Of course, I understand,' she said. 'I sign contracts every day. I'll gladly sign one now, if needed.'

'Then, you understand the unique nature of our approach,' Ian said.

'Naturally,' Victoria said.

'And why it's impossible to make the details public,' Ian said.

'It's only fair,' Victoria said. 'Your terms clearly state that we won't be able to discuss them.'

Victoria's stomach began to complain. Ian gave her a dumb smile, as if she was a lost child. He tapped on his tablet.

'Alright,' he said and turned the screen towards her. 'If you insist.'

Victoria scanned through the text, pausing only on the keywords. Unique system... Own currency... Binding agreement... Legally liable...

'Where do I sign?'

Ian offered a pointy piece of plastic and scrolled to the bottom of the page.

'Now for Mr Evans,' Ian said, pulling the tablet away.

Oliver reached for the tablet.

'Can't I sign for both of us?' Victoria asked.

'Am I to understand that you want to take on the cost for both of you?' Ian asked.

'I'm buying dinner, yes.'

Ian scrolled back up and ticked a box. Victoria added another scribble to the document. Ian gestured to one of the waiters and gave them a smile worthy of a toothpaste advert. The waiter resembled a young Paul Newman.

'Walter, will you show these fine people to their table?'

As Walter led them across the marble floor, they soaked in the subdued elegance of the decor. The dark, wooden tables and designer chairs, the museum-quality abstract paintings, the sense of luxury permeating the room.

'Is that gold?' Oliver pointed at a window knob.

'Stop pointing. You're embarrassing us.'

Their table was perfectly set. A simple porcelain vase with pale pink peonies and white shrubbery stood in the centre. A much-prized Japanese designer's logo was imprinted on the vase. The plates, too, were branded with the same logo.

Walter poured water into the crystal glasses and returned with a bread basket and two shells filled with a scoop of green and brown puree.

'We'll start with the amuse-bouche. Compliments of the house,' he said. 'A young clam on a bed of miso-braised wild mushrooms.'

Every word intensified Oliver's delight. The bread smelled as though it was freshly baked.

'How wonderful,' he said, 'and we haven't even seen the menu.'

Walter opened his mouth but Victoria had already placed her hand on Oliver's knee, her own way of telling him to stop talking.

'My husband likes to joke,' she said. 'We know you work with a tasting menu.'

Walter nodded and extended his hand, as though introducing an orchestra. 'Tonight, we'll prepare seven dishes for you, each paired with a perfect glass of wine. Some people prefer to choose their wine. Both options are included in the price.'

'Perfect pairing sounds lovely, thank you,' Victoria said.

When Walter was far enough away that he could no longer hear them, Oliver leaned closer to his wife.

'I thought you hated tasting menus.'

'Not in a place like this,' she said. 'Did you read any of the things I sent you?'

'I'm sorry, love, I didn't mean to—'

'It's fine,' Victoria said and scooped the last bits of her amuse-bouche from the shell. It was a bite-sized rapture, with a sweetness to it, but also salty with bitter notes at the end. Her stomach begged for more. She had to hold back from shovelling the pieces of bread into her mouth.

For the first time since they arrived, Oliver looked at the other guests. The young woman and man by the window appeared somewhat unglamorous. Their T-shirts were at least two sizes too big and their jeans ripped at the knees. Both wore white sneakers and hand jewellery. Oliver didn't have any strong feelings about fashion - he only had questions. Couldn't young people afford to buy a new pair of trousers?

At the big table in the middle was a party of seven - five adults and two kids. The wrapped boxes and shiny clothes made Oliver believe they were celebrating something. Then, there was a middle-aged man with greasy hair who looked like he hadn't washed his clothes in a while. If Oliver had seen him outside, he'd have taken him for a homeless person, yet there he was, eating his dinner and drinking wine like the rest.

Was this how this kind of place operated? Accepting everyone who came? Oliver would have never considered splashing out like this, especially not since he lost his job, almost a year ago. Victoria had won a major contract, though, and wanted to celebrate. How could he refuse when she worked so hard?

He turned to his wife, surprised to meet her narrowed gaze.

'What is it?' she asked.

'Nothing, love.'

'You have that look.'

'What look?'

'As if something's wrong.'

'Not at all. It's just…'

'Just what?'

In Victoria's eyes, spoiling the mood was a serious crime, so Oliver drank some water.

'I'm glad we're here,' he said.

'You need to trust me more,' Victoria said.

'I do trust you, love.'

He wasn't lying. Oliver possessed neither Victoria's savvy nor her immediate grasp of people and situations, and he knew it.

'How did you enjoy our amuse-bouche?' Walter asked, when he came to collect the empty shells.

'It was divine,' Victoria said.

'I'm glad to hear it,' said Walter, without waiting for Oliver's response. 'We'll continue with tender Brussels sprouts, marinated in balsamic vinegar with fine herbs, accompanied by oven-baked butter cheese with mustard and a glass of Chablis from twenty-eighteen.'

'Marvellous,' Victoria said.

'Did he say Brussels sprouts?' Oliver whispered.

'Marinated in balsamic vinegar, yes.'

'But Brussels sprouts?'

Victoria blinked in the way that made her eyes thunder.

'Stop it,' she said. 'Brussels sprouts are a delicacy, if you know how to prepare them.'

She'd never had such delicate Brussels sprouts herself, but she firmly believed they existed.

Walter returned with a bottle of wine and poured a tasting splash into Victoria's glass. She nodded approvingly. As they sipped their Chablis, he presented them with the Brussels sprouts.

Oliver took the first bite with caution, in case he had to spit it out. Victoria wouldn't approve of this so he'd eat a small bite and leave the rest, but the Brussels sprouts tasted nothing like any vegetable he'd ever had. In fact, they didn't taste like a vegetable at all. The bite on his tongue was tender and salty. Victoria observed him with a raised eyebrow.

'You were right,' Oliver said and took another bite. 'This place *is* different.'

'I wouldn't have tried so hard if it wasn't.'

The plate was empty much faster than Oliver wished. When a different waiter passed their table with Brussels sprouts, Oliver gazed at the plates, awestruck. He waited for Victoria to check her phone, then scooped up the leftover sauce with his finger, licking it off.

'How on earth do they make it taste like this?' he asked.

'I doubt they'll tell us,' Victoria said.

'In one of the articles you sent,' Oliver said, careful not to give away it was the only article he'd read, 'it said Masterson has poached the world's best chefs.'

'He can definitely afford it,' Victoria said.

She tried to appear cool but whenever a dish was carried in their direction, her heart fluttered. She let the wine soften her mouth. The next time she raised her gaze, Walter was carrying fresh plates filled with luxury.

∼

Victoria licked her lips at the thought of the tender duck breast that was no more: its crispy skin and soft flesh, the crunchy cashew-nut crumbs sprinkled over the salty apricot sauce. The burst of pleasure was simply too much to take.

'This was the best bird I've ever had,' Oliver said.

For once, she had to agree. Every dish brought to their table was exceptional, unforgettable even. Sure, she'd expected a high standard, but this?

'We need to come back,' she said. 'Next week, if possible.'

'If they're not booked out.'

'The agreement said you get priority after you've been here, because you don't have to go through all the...'

The words withered in her mouth as she spotted Walter with two plates.

'Our chocolate cake,' Walter said. 'Seventy percent cocoa and a hundred percent pleasure.'

The velvety brown slices were topped with a white dust and accompanied by a yellowish scoop.

'What about the ice cream?' Victoria asked.

'Looks like vanilla,' Oliver said.

'It's yuzu,' Walter said. 'Tart and fragrant to complement the sweetness of the cake.'

'What's yuzu?' Oliver asked.

'It's a type of lemon, like we had in Kyoto.'

'Mrs Evans knows her food,' Walter said.

Victoria beamed. 'Please, call me Victoria.'

Walter poured two glasses of port.

'This fine bottle is from Mr Masterson's private reserve.'

Victoria ate in small bites, wishing the dessert would last longer. The cake, the wine, the whole dinner was too much, but also just enough. Could a person die of too much pleasure? Victoria hoped not, but if she did, at least she'd die happy.

After the cake came the coffee with miniature pink and blue macarons with a green filling. Neither of them felt like having brandy but refusing it would mean they'd have to leave.

'I trust you enjoyed the experience,' Walter asked as he cleared the table.

'Enjoyed? We'll be back tomorrow,' Victoria said.

'Many people say that,' Walter said.

He placed his tablet on the table. 'Shall we confirm the items before I close the account?'

Reluctantly, Victoria scanned over the screen and nodded. As far as she was concerned, the dinner could cost her monthly salary.

'Everything is there,' she said.

'If you could sign here,' Walter said, 'then I'll give you the collector.'

'Oh, of course.'

After she had signed, Walter took away the tablet.

'Don't stare like that,' Victoria said to Oliver. 'He'll think we can't afford it.'

'What's the total?' Oliver asked.

'Does it matter? We have to pay anyway.'

Walter returned with a bill. It was rather short, much like petrol station bills. Victoria made a mental note to borrow the trick. It was always better to make the customer think they hadn't overindulged. She peeked at the bottom of the invoice and blinked.

'That's the total sum?' she asked.

'That's right,' Walter said.

She pointed at the number six on the screen.

'The one here?'

'Using our own currency helps us save paper. Too many zeros can confuse people,' Walter said.

With a blank stare, Victoria reached for her credit card. Whether it was six hundred or six thousand, she'd have to pay it.

'You could easily charge double,' Oliver said.

Walter flashed a smile. 'We don't want to exaggerate. Most people find the price… sufficient.'

'It's not about the money, right?' Oliver said.

'Quite right,' Walter said.

Victoria looked at the device in Walter's hands. It resembled a smart wristwatch with a tiny TV screen. He offered her the device.

'Most people prefer it if we help with putting on the collector,' Walter said.

Victoria cocked an eyebrow, unsure whether the device was a parting gift or a novel way to collect feedback. 'So, how does it work?'

'It's quite simple,' Walter said. 'You put it on your wrist and I'll turn it on. Some people experience a slight itch, but it doesn't hurt.'

A sickness nested in Victoria's stomach. 'How exactly does it... collect?'

She'd never admit to not having read all forty-two pages of the agreement. With a business to run and only two hands, they couldn't expect her to read everything.

Oliver picked up on her discomfort but didn't know what to do.

'If it's not too much trouble,' Victoria asked, 'could you convert the six back to all the zeros? To humour me?'

'Certainly,' Walter said. It seemed to Oliver that he did mind the extra work. They were the last two people in the restaurant.

'That's two tasting menus with wine, the service charge... yes, here it is.'

Walter tapped on his tablet and showed the screen.

'It amounts to a hundred and fifteen thousand times three... times two...'

Oliver gawked at the rows of zeros.

'You understand why we prefer to show days instead of individual heartbeats?'

A speck of dust got stuck in Victoria's throat. She started to cough.

'Are you alright, love?' Oliver asked. 'Here, have some water.'

Victoria fanned the air in front of her face.

'My allergy is acting up,' she said, draining the glass.

'So, the collector will take that?' she asked.

'That's what he said, love.'

'It will collect the total sum, all six days at once,' Walter said.

'Six days of her life,' Oliver said in an attempt to clarify, as if clarity was needed. One look at Victoria's face told him it wasn't.

'Of course, *my* life,' Victoria said. 'I did offer to pay, didn't I?'

She let Walter put the collector around her wrist. Once he closed the clasp, the screen displayed her heartbeat.

'If you refer ten new guests, you get a fifteen percent discount,' Walter said.

'Hear that, sweetheart?' Oliver said, but Victoria didn't want to hear anything. She wanted to crawl into her bed and stare at the ceiling. Instead, she was blinking at the screen of this ridiculous device.

'What do you do with all the heartbeats?' Oliver asked.

'Even if I knew, I couldn't tell you,' Walter said.

'Of course not,' Victoria said. 'Proprietary information.'

The number six appeared on the collector's screen.

'I'm afraid it's safely guarded,' Walter said. 'Not even Mr Masterson's closest circle are privy to this information,' Walter said.

'You mean, no one knows?'

'Except Richard Masterson, I suppose,' Victoria said.

She held her breath, as Walter pressed a small button on the collector. The pressure in her hand increased. She felt like a car tyre about to blow up. The numbers on the screen started to count down to zero. Victoria winced and closed her eyes.

'There,' Walter said and unclasped the device. 'Not too unpleasant, I hope.'

Victoria clenched her teeth and smiled.

'I'll bring your coats,' Walter said, rubbing her hand.

'Did it hurt?'

'Not now, Oliver.'

When Walter offered help with their coats, Victoria took hers and pulled it on, even though her hand was still sore. Walter walked them to the door.

'I hope we've made it worth your time,' he said, 'and that we'll see you soon.'

They walked to their car in silence. Ahead, darkness stretched like an infinite curtain. Alluring. Ravenous.

Oliver said nothing when his wife took the driver's seat. She was in no state to drive, but after losing six days of her life, he could hardly take it away from her. Perhaps driving would help take her mind off the evening.

Victoria kicked off her heels and tossed them into the back seat. Oliver felt the need to talk. If they continued acting as if nothing had happened, a chill would settle between them and wrap every word in frost, like liquid nitrogen.

'How bad was it?' he asked quietly. 'The collector?'

Victoria fiddled with the radio dial. Once more, they were stuck with classical music composed by a Russian.

'He said it might itch,' Oliver said.

Victoria bit into her cheek. Why did Oliver want to discuss this? When they first met, she'd found his attention to detail charming: how he picked up on things others didn't notice. Now, it wore her down.

'It was unpleasant,' she said. 'Like sucking the air out of my veins.'

For a few beats, Oliver said nothing.

'We don't need to go back.'

Victoria added power to the engine.

'Why not? I don't always have to be the one to pick up the check.'

Oliver held his breath. He decided not to say anything. His wife exaggerated when she was upset. What worried him more was the fog that was drifting across the road.

'We're not in a hurry, are we?' he asked.

Victoria clutched onto the wheel. If it was up to her husband, he'd drive in first gear and they'd get home after midnight. Of course, he wasn't the one who had to get up the next morning. It wasn't his life that had got shortened like a pair of trousers.

'I'm tired,' she said. The car jerked as she switched to fourth gear. 'We're alone anyway.'

'For now,' he said.

'We'll see the lights, won't we?'

To put her mind at ease, Victoria started to compose a mental list of all the people she could refer to Moments. Maybe she could even talk some of them into paying for the whole thing. That awful Christina, for example, with her stinky dog that shat all over the lawn, or the accountant from the third floor who made sexual comments whenever he sees a pair of legs.

'Whom would you bring to Moments?' she asked.

Oliver tipped his head to one side, unsure he'd heard right. The fog ahead grew thick, like cream.

'What do you mean?' he asked.

'Your old colleagues. Cousins, aunts, people you know.'

'I'm not sure they'd want to go when they hear about the price,' Oliver said.

'We can't tell them, can we? I signed that paper for both of us.'

The fog drifted on sluggishly, but Victoria wouldn't relent. She refused to be slowed down by something as ridiculous as moisture. The engine was loud enough to scare any beasts away from jumping onto the road.

'Aren't we going a bit fast?' Oliver asked.

Victoria's neck stiffened. The last thing she needed were directions from her husband. She opened her mouth to let out whatever words were broiling inside, when there was a loud plunk and the front of the car plunged into a massive hole filled with rainwater. She tried getting out by pushing the accelerator but the car wouldn't move.

'Well?' Victoria said. 'Aren't you going to check?'

Oliver unbuckled his seatbelt. He got out and circled around the car, shielding his eyes from the headlights. Victoria reached for her phone. She'd had quite enough of this evening. If she got the faintest signal, she'd call her car assistance and let them handle this mess. It was the least they could do with the prices they'd been charging.

There was no signal.

A shadow flickered in the headlights. Victoria looked up and saw Oliver waving at her and shouting something. She couldn't hear what because of the radio, but she assumed he wanted her to get out and look at the mud hole while he'd explain they needed to call someone. The one thing Oliver couldn't do was fix things.

She unbuckled her seatbelt and stretched back between the two front seats to get her shoes. They'd be ruined in the mud, but her annoyance had started to bubble and the only way to put an end to it was to tell Oliver to stop fussing and search for a spot with some signal.

She had to get on all fours to reach the heel of one of her shoes. There was a knock on the window and Oliver's mumbled voice shouted something over the radio.

'For God's sake, Oliver, hold on a sec,' she shouted back.

The knocking continued. She'd finally managed to grab her shoes and was turning around to tell Oliver exactly what she thought when a light blinded her. She entered a white space that pulsed with anguish.

The sharp tang of hand sanitiser absorbed all other smells of the hospital. Oliver rubbed Victoria's hand and wondered how long it would take before it smelled of cream again. He needed to feel Victoria's warmth and see the movement in her chest to remind himself that the worst hadn't happened.

A monitor above her bed displayed her heartbeat. For the second day in a row, Oliver sat by her side and made sure none of the tubes became disconnected and none of the machines stopped working. The doctors and nurses did what they could, but they couldn't be there all the time.

The purple bruises on Victoria's face reminded Oliver of leeches. She looked so small under the white covers. Small and frail. He squeezed her hand. It was limp but warm.

A nurse came in, a different one than the day before. Oliver knew she wouldn't console him, nor would she provide an update. The doctor had told him that after the operation, but his eyes were brimming with hope.

The nurse checked the chart at the footrest of the bed and ran her pencil over the paper. Her lips moved silently. She looked at the monitor and at Victoria.

'Shouldn't she be awake by now?' Oliver asked.

There'd been no news since yesterday. The doctor had said she was stable but they'd have to wait and see.

'She'll come around, don't worry,' the nurse said. She added an extra pillow to the two under Victoria's head, then she scribbled on the chart and hung it back at the footrest.

'The doctor said…' Oliver didn't know how to finish. What could he say? That he needed to know Victoria would make it? That she wouldn't suffer too much when she came around?

'She's recovering,' the nurse said. 'You've got nothing to worry about.'

'What do I do when she wakes up?' Oliver asked.

'Call the doctor,' the nurse said. 'She'll be confused and probably won't remember much.'

'What if she asks what happened?'

'Give her the broad strokes,' the nurse said, 'but no details. Leave those to the doctor. Another shock could send her back.'

'She will come around, though, won't she?'

The nurse gave him a reassuring smile, as if he was asking if he'd still get his Christmas present even though he no longer believed in Santa.

'There was no permanent damage to the head. As for other parts…'

Victoria's hand jerked.

'She's waking up,' said Oliver.

The nurse glanced at the clock on the wall, then at Victoria.

'I'll let the doctor know,' she said. 'She's just finishing up with another patient so it might take some time.'

Victoria's eyes were still closed but her head moved from one side to the other. Her lips moved in a murmur. Oliver sat down on the bed and caressed her face, careful to avoid the bruises.

'What's this?' Victoria shielded her eyes from the light.

Oliver kissed her cheek and then her hands, aware that the next few minutes before the doctor came might be the last he'd spend with his wife as she was.

'I'm right here, darling,' he said.

'Where am I?'

Gently, he moved Victoria's hand away from her face. She blinked and looked around.

'A hospital?'

'One of the best, love. They cured Richard Masterson of cancer…'

Oliver stopped mid-sentence, aware that he shouldn't have mentioned Masterson. It might give Victoria a clue as to what had happened on their way home. Remembering too much could cause a shock.

Victoria tried to prop herself up but the tubes in her arms stopped her. She became aware of the buzzing and beeping sounds of the machines.

'Why am I here?' she asked.

'The doctor will be here any time,' Oliver said. 'She'll explain.'

'Why can't you tell me?'

'There's nothing to worry about,' he said. 'You just rest, get better.'

Victoria pushed away his hand.

'Don't talk to me as if I'm a child.'

She discovered the buttons at the side of her bed, put her headrest up and inspected the room.

'It was the food, wasn't it? I got food poisoning.'

Oliver considered which innocent clues he could provide without giving too much away. If Victoria started to suspect something was wrong, there'd be no way to hide the truth from her. He glanced at the door but the corridor was empty.

'Oliver?' Victoria said. 'Was it the food? I bet it was that clam.'

'It was a good dinner, wasn't it?'

He took away one cushion and placed it on a chair. Then, he puffed up the cushions behind her back, shielding her view of the lower part of the bed.

'The road was bad,' Victoria said.

'The rain didn't help,' he said.

A shadow fell on Victoria's face. She looked away.

'I wanted to get my shoes,' she said, 'but then…'

He squeezed her hand, a bit too hard.

'Watch out!'

'Sorry, love.' He kissed her hand. How much longer would the doctor need?

'There were lights,' she said. 'Hurting my eyes.'

'Would you like some water?' Oliver asked. 'Or food? You must be hungry. I'll ask the nurse to bring a snack.'

As he poured water into a glass, he wondered how much Victoria remembered. She couldn't have heard him calling to switch off the high beams. If she had, none of this would have happened. Oliver placed the glass of water into her hands.

'Our car,' she said. 'Where is it?'

'It's being taken care of,' he said. 'Don't you worry.'

Technically, this wasn't a lie – he'd ordered the same model and colour. The old one would be of little use after they'd had to cut a hole in it to get Victoria out.

He stood up. 'The important thing is that you're recovering. The doctor said that in a few months…'

'Months!'

Victoria's hand twitched and she spilled the water into her lap. It took Oliver a moment too long to notice that it was spreading down her legs: down where her legs used to be. The outline of the stumps just below her knees became clear. Victoria's eyes widened. She started to breathe fast, as if she was running.

'Take it off,' she said.

'Don't be upset, love.'

'Take the bloody thing off!'

Her hands shook as she pulled the side of the blanket but it didn't move because it was tucked in.

'Oliver!'

The empty glass tumbled off the bed and broke into pieces.

'The doctor said you shouldn't...'

'Take it off!'

Oliver's throat felt like a grater, shredding each word before it reached the tongue. He didn't dare look at Victoria's legs.

'It was structural damage,' he said.

The machine above Victoria's head started to beep faster. She dug her fingernails into his arm.

'My legs!'

If he lied to her, she'd resent him for the rest of their lives.

'The engine,' he said. 'It was pushed forward when the other car hit ours. You were unbuckled, so...'

Victoria's wail sounded like a siren. Colour returned to her cheeks but it reminded him of the blood she'd lost. He could explain to her that things would work out, that nothing had to change, but she'd read the lie right off his face.

'The doctor will tell you about the options,' he said. 'How we can make things easier.'

'I'm a cripple!'

Victoria's voice carried across the room into the corridor. Oliver hoped the doctor would hurry.

'Darling,' he said, 'we'll get through this.'

'We? Easy for you to say. Just look at me! I should have died.'

'Don't say that.'

'I'd rather be dead than a cripple.'

'You're not a cripple. You're a wonderful person and you deserve...'

Victoria shook her head and cried harder. 'I should have died.'

Pieces tore out of Oliver's chest, even parts he considered unbreakable. In all the years of their marriage, he'd seen Victoria cry twice: the first time when her mother died and the second time when she found their three-day-old son cold in his crib. She didn't deserve this. Richard Masterson, on the other hand...

The thought of the wealthy mogul stirred up fire in Oliver's guts. Why was he out driving that late anyway? Didn't he own a helicopter? Didn't he have a restaurant to run, women to chase, heartbeats to collect?

Oliver's fingers balled into a fist.

'I'll be a stone around your neck,' Victoria cried. 'A burden!'

'You'll never be a burden, love,' he said and meant it. 'You'll walk again, you'll see. It will just take some time. I'll do anything I can to help.'

He wished he'd taken notes when the doctor had first explained Victoria's options.

'I should fall down the stairs and break my neck, like Grandpa in his wheelchair.'

Victoria paused, as though she'd thought of something. 'You'll do anything?'

'Anything,' Oliver said.

'You'll take me to Moments?'

'Love?'

'I'll eat there every day, till my days run out,' she said. 'I'll bring the whole office and foot the bill. How long do I have, do you think, before I reach zero?'

Oliver pressed the red button at the bedside. 'Why don't you rest a bit, love. When you get out, we can go somewhere nice. I could book that hotel you liked, by the beach.'

Victoria's face lit up. 'Book it, Oliver. Book it and drown me there.'

Oliver pressed the red button one more time and held Victoria close. She muttered something, but her mouth was pressed against his chest so he couldn't hear what she was saying. He didn't want to, either.

She pushed him away. 'If you won't help me, I'll do it myself,' she said, 'like I have to do everything else myself.'

At that moment, the doctor pushed the door open and marched into the room.

'I tried, Doctor,' Oliver said. 'I really did.'

The last thing Oliver heard, as he was ushered out of the room, was Victoria repeating the same sentence.

'I married a wimp, Doctor,' she said. 'I married a wimp.'

Victoria's words ricocheted off the sterile walls and the polished hospital floor. She couldn't have meant what she'd said, thought Oliver as he stared at the brown liquid trickling out of the vending machine. It was the shock, the anger talking.

The doctor would explain everything, calm Victoria down and convince her that her life wasn't over. As much as Oliver wanted to believe this, he also knew how stubborn his wife could be.

He paced up and down the corridor and drank the vile-tasting coffee. If only they'd never gone to Moments. How could he stop Victoria from taking her own life by eating there? Could he convince Richard Masterson to ban her from his restaurant? It would be the least he could do after his flashy SUV had squashed Victoria's legs. Masterson had got away with a mild concussion and a broken arm. Even if there had been a more serious injury, the man's future was secured with the heartbeats. A man like Richard Masterson could live forever.

Oliver paused in front of a lift. Hadn't one of the doctors mentioned a suite on the fourth floor? It must have been where they kept Masterson, possibly guarded by special security. God forbid that anyone would shorten the man's sleep by even a second.

Out of the corner of his eye, Oliver spotted two doctors coming out of the staff room. He'd seen people come in and out before at the end of shifts.

He tossed the empty coffee cup into the bin and bought another. If he stuck around, more doctors would enter the staff room. He waited for the right moment, then rushed to put his foot between the door and the post.

Once inside the staff room, Oliver searched the closets. The room was empty but anyone could come in at any moment, so Oliver grabbed the first coat he saw. It wasn't a fresh one but it had a tag on it that said Dr Nathan Wesley, Neurosurgeon. He put it on.

The elevator took him to the fourth floor. He checked the corridor, then found a room with Masterson's name.

His heart thudded as he closed the door behind him. The room was much bigger and better equipped than Victoria's, with a bath, a big table and four chairs. Richard Masterson lay on his side. His broken arm was in a cast and his hand clutched around a remote control. His other hand was under a pillow. He was deeply asleep, possibly thanks to an expensive drug cocktail.

If Oliver woke him up, Masterson would need some time before he'd be able to understand him. What if he called security? Oliver had no means to fight against people of Masterson's stature. Then again, what choice did he have? No one else knew how this damned restaurant worked, the waiter had been quite clear about that.

And if Masterson wouldn't help him?

Oliver slumped onto the pillows that were stacked in an armchair and exhaled loudly. He couldn't blow this chance. He might not get another one. Only Richard Masterson could help him, no one else.

Oliver's gaze shifted and his chin dropped. A thought stuck in his mind and made his skin tingle.

No one else could do it but Richard Masterson. If anything happened to him, they'd have to close Moments down. Victoria had always said Masterson was a vain man so it was unlikely he'd shared his secret, or heartbeats, with anyone else. No one else knew how to collect heartbeats.

Could he? Should he?

Oliver stood up and drew the curtains around the bed. He turned around and felt the pillows on the armchair. They were fuller, sturdier than Victoria's.

Richard Masterson's chest rose and fell as Oliver tiptoed over to his bed.

I'm not a wimp, thought Oliver as he gripped the sides of the pillow. He'd prove it.

Slowly, he raised his hands. As he brought the pillow down onto the man's face, Oliver imagined the collected heartbeats racing down to zero.

MY FRIEND BETTY

From afar, the house drooped like a willow tree but the surrounding landscape made up for it. The light green grass glowed like an emerald and the daisy blossoms bobbed in the wind. Fiona squinted to take it all in.

'Look, Mummy. Trees!'

Before Fiona could react, her daughter ran towards the orchard, clutching onto her plush bunny.

'Not so fast, Mandy!'

It was a half-hearted warning: Mandy must have felt it, for she didn't stop. There was only a meadow, trees and the house next door. It'd be a change from the city and their small flat in the centre. It wouldn't be the only change.

After Fiona had caught up with her daughter, they lay down in the grass and inhaled the moist, sweet air. The deep green leaves on the trees glistened with dew and the sky was blue and open.

When they returned to the house, Fiona glanced at the overgrown yard, lost in shrubbery and thorns. She'd have to tear it all out, plant a few things and shape the hedges. By summer, the house would become an enchanted villa. She'd sell it for double what she'd paid.

It was the inside she worried about. Once she removed all the clutter, the house would look decent enough but a fresh lick of paint wouldn't fix the sombre atmosphere. There were spaces in the house that the light couldn't reach. The living room was gloomy and didn't warm up, no matter how often Fiona opened the windows.

Then, there was the kitchen. Despite all the cleaning, the space looked tarnished, like an old piece of jewellery, unloved and forgotten. It must have been why the price had been so low.

'Look, Mummy! This tree is bigger than I am!'

Mandy wrapped her hands around an old oak, dancing around it.

'Careful, Mandy. You'll get a splinter.'

Mandy went on for a while, then sat down.

'Why isn't Daddy here?' she asked.

Fiona swallowed the air.

'You know why, pumpkin.'

'Because he's somewhere else?'

Suddenly, Mandy's wide eyes seemed too much. Too blue, too inquisitive, too much like Rob's.

'We talked about this, remember?' Fiona said.

'Because he's in heaven now?'

'That's right, pumpkin.'

Fiona dropped her gaze and took Mandy's hand. Despite her effort to push back the salt in her throat, a teardrop slid down her cheek. She wiped it with her sleeve.

'Don't be sad, Mummy. He might come back.'

Fiona put on her stern face. She wouldn't cry. Not again, not here. She thought about saying something about the bunny when a shadow cut through the light. When Fiona turned, she saw two figures coming closer: a tall one and a small one. Fiona shielded her eyes. They were holding hands. A woman and a child. The woman was smiling.

'I'm sorry,' the woman said.

She looked younger than Fiona and carried a plastic bag that smelled of peppers.

'I wanted to come a bit later, but Ben couldn't wait to meet the new neighbours. Excuse him. It's been a long time since anyone else lived here.'

'That's alright,' Fiona said. 'We're still unpacking, so I hope you don't mind the mess.'

It was a lie, but she couldn't tell the truth either. Unpacking would mean she'd have to open the boxes and face the leftovers of her life. She'd have to unpack Rob's stuff, drag out things she'd tried so hard to shut away. She'd finally come to the stage where she didn't cry every day.

The woman stretched out her hand. 'I'm Meg. We live over there.'

The house at the other end of the orchard was small and cute and looked like a house Fiona would buy, if it wasn't that far out.

She shook Meg's hand. 'Fiona. And this is my...'

Mandy didn't wait to be introduced. She'd dragged the boy and her bunny to the oak and sat down. Fiona forgot what she wanted to say. There were fewer dangers here than in the city. Besides, the boy probably knew the yard better than they did.

She caught Meg's expectant gaze.

'I'm sorry, it's just still all...'

Scary? Lonely?

'New,' Fiona said. 'We're used to the city.'

Fiona gestured at the grey metal chairs that had once been white and they say down.

'I shouldn't forget these.' Meg put the plastic bag on the table. 'They're for you. Fresh peppers and tomatoes from our garden.'

'Thank you,' Fiona said. 'That's very kind.'

'Ben and I can only eat so much. Especially now he's in this phase of eating only specific colours. Red and green are alright, but not yellow.'

Fiona laughed.

'How old is he?'

'Five.'

'Mandy's four.'

They turned to the kids, who were deep into a role-play.

'Life's easy for them, hey?' Meg said.

'I almost forgot that it can be.'

Fiona hadn't meant to blurt this out, not in front of a complete stranger. Talking to strangers was nice, though. There was no pity in their eyes. Fiona's friends dispensed it like medicine. It made everything taste bitter.

Meg must have sensed something in Fiona's voice, for she leaned forwards and smiled at her. 'We're planning a barbecue this weekend. Nothing fancy, some grilled vegetables, chicken, cookies, if Ben doesn't eat them all before then. We'd love it if you and Mandy could join.'

Fiona was about to reply when Mandy shouted from the distance.

'Mummy! Ben's got a pirate ship. Can I play at his house?'

They laughed.

'I suppose that's a yes,' Fiona said.

'I need to check on my bread, anyway.' Meg waved to Ben but he pretended not to notice.

'I could bring him over, if you like. Not sure Mandy will let him go. She's quite stubborn.'

Fiona stopped herself from saying, 'Like her dad'.

'Oh, would you mind?'

'Not at all.'

'I'm happy to return the favour,' Meg said. 'If there's anything I can do to help…'

As Meg turned towards the house, a shadow fell on her face. It occurred to Fiona that if Meg had finished the thought, she wouldn't have made an offer. She'd have given a warning.

'Come on, pumpkin. Put on the shoes.'

It had taken Fiona the whole morning to get Mandy ready for her play date. After the initial enthusiasm had worn off, Mandy seemed less keen on spending time with Ben. Fiona's patience was waning.

Mandy sat on the floor and clutched her plush bunny.

'Not these,' Mandy said. 'I want my wellies with daisies.'

Fiona tried to coax Mandy's foot into the sandal. 'Wellies are for the rain. It's sunny today.'

Mandy crossed her arms. 'I want daisies.'

'They're still caked in mud. You don't want to make Meg's house dirty, do you?'

'Betty says daisies are better,' Mandy said.

Fiona fastened the first sandal onto her daughter's foot. She took up the second one, but Mandy pushed her leg firmly against the floor.

'Don't you mean Ben?'

'No, Mummy, Betty. You need to listen.'

'Who's Betty?'

'Betty is my friend. We play every day.'

After fiddling with the sandal, Fiona strapped it onto Mandy's foot. What she really wanted was to sleep. All the work had been exhausting and she struggled to sleep. It was as though this place didn't want her here. No wonder her daughter had invented a friend to cope with it.

'You'll have to introduce me to her. When is she coming to visit?'

Mandy stood up and rolled her eyes. 'Betty doesn't visit, Mummy. She lives here.'

Fiona's chest rattled. Mandy's imagination was acting up. Another thing she'd got from her father.

'How handy. You can play with her any time.'

'Not any time. Only in the morning and before I go to bed.'

'What does Betty do during the day?'

'Sleeping.'

Fiona exhaled loudly. She was too tired to appreciate Mandy's creativity in whipping up excuses. In the morning, Mandy took ages to get ready and later, she couldn't get her to go to sleep. Still, she insisted she wanted to sleep in her own room.

'Alright, pumpkin. Shall we go to Ben's?'

Mandy nodded and ran off, as if it had been Meg who was keeping her from going there. If things went well, Fiona could finish the front yard and repaint the bathrooms. But, after she'd dropped Mandy off, she had little energy left and had to lie down to recuperate.

Her grief counsellor had told her she'd have to take it a day at a time. As much as Fiona tried, there were days with little light, days when she wished it was she, not Rob, who had died in that accident.

Still, by the evening, she had finished a fair amount of work, enough to earn some time to herself. In the city, she could have gone out, taken Mandy to the spa or to the cinema. Here, though, the best she could do was drink her coffee out in the sun and watch Ben and Mandy play.

Later, after Mandy had gone to bed, Fiona heard a murmur behind her daughter's door. The lights were off, but Mandy wasn't sleeping. Fiona leaned her ear against the door.

Mandy giggled. 'Don't be mean, Betty. She does *not* talk like that.'

After a moment of silence, Mandy spoke again.

'She'll be scared if I tell her. Ben wouldn't like that, either.'

If Fiona hadn't been so shattered, she'd check on Mandy and read her a story. Mandy had been quick to say goodnight, though. Ever since Rob had died, her little girl had started to close up. She didn't come to sleep with her as often as before, as if she'd built a world of her own and preferred to stay there.

Fiona dragged her heavy feet to her bedroom. Before she closed her eyes, she imagined a house she would buy once she'd sold this one off. It'd be a small place filled with light. The only thing she'd have to worry about would be to remember to buy milk.

The sun changed everything. Daffodils popped out against the blue skies and the once overgrown yard was now a neat garden. Fiona was tending her lilies and monitoring Ben and Mandy, who were making mud pies.

Tending the garden kept dark thoughts at bay. There had been plenty these past weeks. They'd come roaring as if they'd been hiding this whole time. The house was almost ready to be shown. Once she'd sold it, she could move back to the city or a small town nearby, a place where there'd be libraries, spas and cafés.

Still, Fiona didn't want to upset Mandy. She'd got used to their new home and would probably be reluctant to move. Once things were certain and she'd got an offer, she'd break the news.

After finishing weeding the garden, Fiona made lemonade and fished a few cookies out of the jar. Ben and Mandy were running around the yard, but as soon as they saw her carrying a plate, Mandy shrieked with joy.

'Cookies!' She reached for the plate.

'Wash your hands first,' Fiona said.

'I'll have a cookie.'

'Not before you wash your hands.'

'I want one now!'

'You can wash them over there.' Fiona pointed at a small tap she used to water the garden. 'Don't forget to use soap.'

As she watched Mandy and Ben scuttle away, her eyes stopped on a doll that was lying on the ground. It was old and covered in dirt. After Mandy had washed her hands, she wanted to pick it up.

'Leave the doll to rest for a bit,' Fiona said.

'But she'll catch a cold and get sick.'

'We'll draw a nice bath for her, alright?'

This satisfied Mandy. They ate the cookies and drank the lemonade. Mandy tried to snap up the last cookie.

'Na-a,' Fiona said. 'There's dinner soon and we've had quite enough.'

Mandy blinked and made a sad face. Another thing she had in common with her father. Had. Fiona's chest tightened.

'You've had enough, Mandy.'

'It's not for me,' Mandy said. 'It's for Betty.'

Fiona could tell she'd lost the fight so she let Mandy take the last cookie. She didn't eat it, though. She pocketed it.

This imaginary friend thing was getting out of hand. If Fiona sold the house by summer, then they could find a new home by fall.

The pulsing sensation in the pit of Fiona's stomach egged her on. She couldn't quite explain where the thought had come from or why, but it touched her ear like a whisper.

By fall, it might be too late.

The doll gave Fiona the creeps. Mandy had hauled it from who knows where, insisting it was a present from her friend Betty. How had she even got into the cellar? Maybe she'd dug up the doll in the yard. It was certainly filthy enough and had a rotten, dank stink.

After she'd scrubbed it with soap, Fiona disinfected the fractured parts on the doll's fingers and legs. Its black hair was burnt at the edges and parts had been cut off. The doll's hands and legs squeaked when moved. The eyes were the worst, though. They were green and creepy and they closed with a delay, as if the doll was watching her.

Fiona turned it over and left it to soak in the water but seeing the doll with its face down upset Mandy. She told Fiona the doll couldn't breathe and that Betty would be upset if she found out. Bloody Betty. These days, Mandy used her imaginary friend as an excuse for anything. Especially if she wanted another piece of cake or a cookie.

'Betty likes cookies,' Mandy said.

Fiona didn't argue. She barely had the energy to get out of bed at the moment. If an extra cookie or a piece of chocolate bought her peace, so be it. Except for her friendship with Betty, Mandy was a reasonable child. Too reasonable. She'd got that from Fiona, or at least Fiona hoped so.

Fiona's shoulders tensed as she descended into the basement. The last thing to do was to clear away the rubbish left by the previous owner. An old lady, the estate agent had said, who didn't have anyone else left. After having the plumbing and the floorboards fixed, Fiona wanted to save some money. She'd clear the basement herself. How hard could it be to ditch those boxes?

The deep, musty smell made her queasy. Fiona turned on a light, a single bulb hanging from a piece of cord. She stepped over the rusty floor drain and tried to overlook the thick layers of dust.

Holding her breath, Fiona counted the boxes. There were eighteen, plus a few old cans of paint, brushes and a ladder. Her throat knotted. The bolted windows were too high to reach. She couldn't open them without using the ladder, which didn't seem all that safe.

Fiona had no intention of touching things without rubber gloves on. She'd make an estimate of stuff to get rid of, then fetch a bucket and bleach and a gazillion rubbish bags. She'd have asked Meg to help her, but she dared not bring her friend into this suffocating place.

A ray of sunlight cut through the darkness, making the specks of dust rise and dance. A peculiar sensation came over Fiona that someone was watching her. She shook her head. This was silly. The only living thing, apart from her, was the mildew. Even the spiders were all pale and shrivelled, hanging from their webs.

She pushed a box with her foot. Something moved and Fiona's heart kicked. She rushed towards the stairs, then stopped midway. Everything was still. Maybe it was just a rat. It would be better to hire a professional, ask them to burn things, if they had to. She couldn't risk having rats and mice running around when prospective buyers came to check the house.

Her breath deepened as she climbed the stairs. There was nothing to be frightened of, except the invisible eyes that followed her long after she'd shut the door.

This is nice, thought Fiona as she stretched her feet closer to the fireplace. Meg's house was warm and cosy. The furniture was old and didn't match, but there was a sense of home and comfort, something Fiona hadn't felt in a while.

It's grief, she reassured herself, a concoction of chemicals her body was producing. Why exactly, Fiona couldn't tell, but it seemed to her that the wavering moods, the unexpected bursts of emotion were a tactic. If she didn't know what to expect, she had no choice but to keep going.

'More wine?'

Meg didn't wait for Fiona's answer before topping up her glass. The Cabernet tasted smooth and heavy and wrapped around Fiona's mind in all the right places.

'No, *I* am the pirate with an eye-patch!' Mandy shouted from Ben's room.

Fiona was leaning forwards to put down her glass when Meg stopped her.

'Relax,' Meg said. 'Debbie will take care of it. She's a great sitter.'

Fiona exhaled and leaned back. Where had the time gone? The summer was almost over and she hadn't finished renovating. The roof leak was not fixed – she'd have to change the broken tiles. This past week had felt like a month and Mandy's growing demands didn't help.

At least she'd stopped dragging along that dreadful doll. Fiona had bribed her with a cup of hot chocolate and a few biscuits, which Mandy claimed were for Betty.

'You seem tired.' Meg curled her legs up.

'This is my night out,' Fiona said. 'I'm usually in bed by nine.'

'Cheers,' Meg raised her glass. 'We should have a proper night out, though.'

'Where? I guess we could move the table into the orchard.'

Meg laughed.

'No, I mean in town. My friend is having a small party next Friday.'

'I don't know,' Fiona said. 'I wouldn't want to drive back in the middle of the night, and—'

'We could crash in her spare room. There'd probably be a few more of us, but they're nice people. What do you say?'

Fiona swirled the wine around her glass.

'What about Mandy?'

Meg cocked an eyebrow and smiled.

'We can ask Debbie. I'm sure she won't mind. She's going to babysit Ben anyway.'

'So, you're definitely going?'

'I need it. Come on. How long since you've been out with just adults?'

Too long to remember, thought Fiona. She took another sip.

'It's not that easy.'

'You've hardly left the house since you moved in. If anything, there is...'

Meg paused, as though she'd changed her mind.

'There's something wrong with it, isn't there?' Fiona asked.

Meg's gaze shifted. Perhaps she didn't want to talk about the house, but the air was already tainted, the pleasant atmosphere punctured.

They took a generous sip of Cabernet.

'There's always something wrong when a house is as old as yours.'

'You aren't talking about cracked pipes and poor roofing, are you?'

Meg's jaw tensed. There was a slight change in her tone, too.

'Why? Did anything happen?' Meg asked.

'I don't know. It's a weird place. Sometimes, I feel…'

Looking at Meg, she paused. Could she say she felt as if she was being watched? By whom? There was no one else for miles around. She didn't want to imply that Meg was somehow spying on her.

'You feel what?' Meg asked.

Fiona sighed and drank more wine. 'Lonely.'

She wasn't lying, either.

'More reasons to go out and have some fun, hey? At least think about it.'

'Alright.'

'Promise?'

Fiona raised her glass. 'We need a refill.'

As Meg fetched the bottle, Fiona thought about the guy she'd hired to empty the basement. He'd arrived whistling, had coffee with her and told her all about his twins and their new puppy. After he'd finished, he'd barely stopped to say goodbye. His cheeks had been leached of colour, his eyes absent.

'Who lived there before me?' Fiona asked.

Meg pressed her lips together as she topped up her glass. 'Wendy. She used to be a dancer, jazz ballet and whatnot, but she had a few injuries and had to stop.'

'How old was she?'

Meg sat down. 'Only a bit younger than the house. Seventy-two, I think.'

'I bet the house didn't help with her health. It's cold and damp.'

'Wendy didn't mind.'

Meg wanted to say more when they heard Ben and Mandy shriek. It wouldn't be too long before they called for them to check out what they'd made. If Fiona wanted to find out about the house, she'd have to ask now.

'Mandy found a doll. Must have been Wendy's. She didn't have kids, did she?'

'No, but she had a twin sister. Elizabeth.'

'No longer alive, I suppose?'

'The poor thing died when they were little. Such a sad story, too.'

A bead of sweat slid down Fiona's back like an ice-cold fingertip.

'What happened?'

'Wendy wasn't sure. They were running around and she thought she heard her mum call for cookies. Betty ran down the stairs, fell and broke her neck. She was only seven, the poor thing.'

Fiona swallowed hard. In the other room, Ben and Mandy clapped their hands.

'Mum! Come and see!' Ben said.

'We found treasure,' Mandy said.

Meg put down her wine glass.

'A strange thing,' Fiona said, holding onto her glass. 'Mandy has been asking for cookies lately. Says they're for Betty.'

Meg opened her mouth, then promptly closed it. Ben and Mandy ran into the living room, holding a bunch of Legos put together.

'Whatever she asks for,' Meg said, 'don't say no.'

Fiona dropped her trowel. She had sprayed the plants with insecticide. Still, the lice persisted. Her lilies had been eaten by mites and the other flowers were full of baby lice. The pests had spread all over the garden and she had no energy to deal with them.

Her shirt was soaked in sweat and her hat wasn't much help against the scorching sun. The place was not the luscious paradise she'd imagined. Instead, it was dry, unbearably hot and the soil was too poor to grow any vegetables.

She checked the time. Soon, Meg would bring the kids and she wasn't done with her work. Fiona wiped the sweat off her forehead, dug out the flowers and scooped them into a rubbish bag. A few bushes had survived, so the garden would still be lovely. As she took the bag to the rubbish bin, she spotted a pale, round thing lying in the grass. A paper plate, as it turned out, with a few chocolate cookies.

Ants were crawling all over them. Fiona binned the plate and the cookies. Who would have left food out there and why? It was never a good idea to attract insects. The place was crawling with them and she preferred it if they stayed outside.

Had it been a hiker? Fiona would have noticed anyone who wasn't Meg, Mandy or Ben. As she carried the rubbish to the bin, Fiona considered why the cookies had been left at the back of the house. Maybe they weren't meant to be found? The only other person who could have left the plate was Meg, but why would she do that?

As she returned to the yard, she spotted Meg coming over with the kids, carrying a duffel bag.

'Hey,' Fiona said and gave her a hug.

'Thanks, babe. You're a star.'

'Don't mention it. How long will you be gone?'

'I should be back soon after dinner.'

'No worries,' Fiona said. 'Hope you'll manage to sort things out.'

Meg gave a tired smile. 'He always does that. Barges into my life, makes a mess, then takes off.'

'Is this his stuff?' Fiona asked.

'The last of it. After that…' Meg shrugged.

'Take care.'

Fiona squeezed Meg's shoulder. She didn't have any advice about men. As much as she wanted to ask Meg about the cookies, this wasn't the right time. Meg checked her wristwatch.

'Right,' she said. 'What am I forgetting?'

'We'll be fine,' Fiona said. 'It's green and red for Ben?'

'Anything, if you put it in a toasty,' Meg said before disappearing down the road.

In the evening, Fiona's limbs felt like lead. She'd scrapped her initial idea to make pasta. Ben and Mandy seemed happy enough playing with the bunny. Ben even picked up the creepy doll a few times and tried to make it pretty.

Fiona made cheese sandwiches and put them in the grill sandwich maker. She cut a few of Meg's tomatoes and served them on the plate. Ben grabbed a piece.

'First, we wash our hands.'

Fiona took the kids to the bathroom. When they came back, Ben attacked the food. Not Mandy, though.

'What is it, pumpkin? You've always liked cheese sandwiches.'

'Betty wants a steak,' Mandy said.

'I'm sure Betty can cook her own steak,' Fiona said.

'Betty doesn't cook,' Mandy said. 'She doesn't know how to.'

'Well then.'

Fiona bit into her sandwich, hoping this would end the discussion about Betty.

'Don't be rude, Mummy. Betty wants to eat with us.'

'I thought Betty only ate cookies and came when you go to bed?'

'She's hungry more often, now,' Mandy said.

'Eat your dinner, Amanda.'

Mandy folded her arms. 'I won't, if you don't make something for Betty.'

Fiona curled her toes. She'd toss the doll away first thing tomorrow morning. Without the doll, her daughter would forget about Betty and all her ridiculous demands.

'We don't have a steak,' Fiona said.

Mandy shook her head. 'You can't leave Betty hungry!'

'She can have a slice of tomato. How about that?'

'Betty doesn't like vegetables.'

'Well, that's too bad. Eat your dinner because there won't be anything else till breakfast.'

'But, but—'

'No buts, no ifs. Now, eat your food.'

When Fiona came to tuck her in, Mandy pretended to be asleep. That girl could hold a grudge, just like her father. Her eyelashes trembled when Fiona kissed her on the cheek.

'Night, pumpkin,' she said.

Mandy didn't answer.

Fiona wanted to cuddle up next to her daughter, feel the warmth of her chest rising and falling, but she badly needed to crawl into her bed and drink the last bit of wine to help her fall asleep.

An hour later, she lay in her bed, her door slightly ajar so she'd hear Mandy if she woke up. Fiona's eyelids were heavy, but sleep wouldn't come. The shadows of the trees in the yard moved with the gusts of wind. They reminded Fiona of long hands reaching out.

Soon, her mind softened enough to begin to drift. She'd almost slipped into dreams when the light in the corridor shifted. A shadow in the door was shaped like a person. Not a person, a child.

'Mandy?' Fiona asked.

The shadow moved closer. When Fiona blinked, she saw a small girl in a green dress. She was pale. Her neck was bent to one side. Her dark eyes glowed.

Fiona tried to scream but found it impossible. She struggled to breathe. The girl put her hand on the bed and opened her mouth. With all the tiny teeth, it resembled a shark's jaw. The darkness in the middle expanded. Fiona didn't close her eyes, yet everything she saw was the same colour. Black.

THE RECIPE

Mum lays a platter full of cakes out on the table. Even at sixty, she's made her usual Christmas bake. The lemony cookies that melt on your tongue, the cinnamon rolls and the puffy sponge cake, a yummy cloud of happiness. There's Christmas bread, too.

'Your favourite,' she says, 'with almonds and dried figs.'

It was, till my doctor said no more, but I don't have the heart to tell her that, so I take a morsel and dip it into my tea. A few pieces crumble and sink, sprinkling powdered sugar onto the tablecloth.

'Tomorrow, I'll make an orange crumble. New recipe,' Mum says. Is she apologising for not making enough? She knows some of my friends stayed behind at the campus and I considered it too, but I just couldn't do it. Despite everything that has happened, the thought of Mum alone with her Christmas bake is too much to bear.

'It's fine, Mum.'

Her love always came through food. She baked when she was happy. When she wasn't, you could taste that, too. Dad always got a cookie with his coffee, or just coffee, if she was upset with him. Then, there was the apricot pie. Dad's favourite. Mum would make it for his birthday or to cheer him up.

I examine the red tablecloth with golden snowflake prints. It's barely visible under all the plates and trays. The number of cookies is exactly the same as it was when there were still four of us.

My eyes escape towards the empty seat across the table. In front of it is a small plate with a single heart-shaped butter cookie. The bitter feeling in my mouth expands. I take another piece of bread to stamp it out. No matter how hard I try not to think about Sally, seeing her favourite cookie takes me back there. It was her death that changed everything.

Mum stood in front of Sally's door in her apron, her hands clasped.

'But you love macaroni and cheese!' Mum said.

'I'm not hungry!' Sally said.

The 'KEEP OUT' sign stared back, mocking us.

Dad's heavy steps echoed in the corridor. I hid behind Mum as the music from behind Sally's door grew louder.

'She won't say what's wrong,' Mum said, her voice softened by tears.

'Open up, Sally! That's no way to talk to your mother. And turn that down. You're scaring your little sister.'

'It's called industrial,' Sally shouted. As the volume of the music became unbearable, despair was painted over Mum's face.

'She's already skipped lunch,' Mum said.

The vein on Dad's neck stood out, just like it did when we were running late and the car wouldn't start. He hit the door several times with the palm of his hand in rapid succession.

'That's enough, Sally. You will come out or I'll take that lock off your door.'

After a few moments, the music subsided and the door was flung opened. Out came Sally in her skinny jeans, dark makeup and her washed-out black T-shirt with the big skull. The over-stretched fabric hung off her thin pale limbs.

She sulked at the table as we ate and pushed the macaroni around her plate, as though it was a contestant in a race.

'You're not leaving until you've eaten something,' Dad said.

'I made cookies, too,' Mum said.

'She can have them *after* she's had dinner,' Dad said.

The first bite of Mum's macaroni and cheese wiped the frown right off Sally's face. In the end, she always cleaned the plate and disappeared into her room with a bowl full of Mum's cookies.

'You think she'll be okay?' Mum asked Dad.

'It's a teen thing,' Dad said. 'She'll snap out of it.'

I was only seven, then, and thought that 'a teen thing' was a virus and all Sally needed was some tea and rest.

If I'd known, would things have been any different?

'Do you think it's going to snow on New Year's Eve?' Mum asks.

On the sofa, Snowball pricks his ears up. He was a mere kitten when Mum found him, a tiny ball of white fluff that meowed and followed her around. Now, Snowball is so big that when he stretches across the sofa, there's barely space for anyone else to sit.

'He likes being outside but it's too cold for him now,' Mum says.

She plants a kiss on top of Snowball's head and he presses his furry head against her before resuming his sofa throne position.

'He doesn't look that keen on going out,' I say.

I take another sip of my tea. The cake crumbs dance at the bottom of my cup. I move it and watch them swirl.

'Are you going to the fireworks?' I ask and immediately regret it.

It was Dad who liked them but he's gone now. A knot in my stomach tightens. I try to wash it down with more tea.

'I don't think so. It's too cold,' Mum says.

She gets up and starts rummaging through the cupboard.

'I've made you some jam. You still like blueberry, don't you?'

'Thanks, Mum. You didn't have to.'

Her thin arms fold around me and hold on for a few moments after I let go. She's lost weight. These past years can't have been easy for her. First Sally, then Dad. We never talk about Dad.

~

Sally stood in the middle of the room with her arms crossed, her face flushed.

'But my throat hurts,' she said.

'Fresh air will do you good, sweetheart,' Mum said. 'Remember what the doctor said.'

'I didn't even finish my monies!'

Monies was what Sally called her drawings of dragons, misshapen creatures and mythical monsters.

'Take them with you. There's no law against drawing in the mountains,' Dad said.

Sally looked at Mum as if she expected her to say something, then grabbed her sketchbook and pencils and shoved them into the rucksack.

'I made tuna mayo sandwiches,' Mum said.

A pang of envy pinched my chest as I watched Dad pack spare clothes and a thermos with fresh tea.

'Put on your hiking boots,' Mum said to Sally.

'I wanna go, too. Why can't I go, Mummy?' I said.

'You'll go when you're a bit bigger, Daphne,' Mum said.

'There are big rocks there, pumpkin. You don't want to get hurt. Besides, someone has to stay home and take care of Mum,' Dad said.

He winked at me and they left. I envied Sally so much back then. It seems so absurd, now that I know the truth.

~

For a few moments, Mum stops her exploration of the cupboards and turns to me.

'Maybe you used it up,' I say.

She shakes her head. Her eyes stop at the empty seat with the heart-shaped cookie and a shadow drops onto her face. It awakens a hollow hunger that threatens to swallow us both.

It's hard not to think about Sally. So many times, I've wanted to ask Mum if she kept any of her monies or if she got rid of them, like she got rid of Dad's things. In our house, memories cling to objects like clothes to wet skin. I can't blame Mum for not wanting to collapse under their weight.

'Mum?'

'Yes, love?'

The silence closes in on me once again. It's cold and harsh, like armour that you can't take off. I've grown accustomed to it. If I tried to break it, Mum and I could no longer walk around the gaping void between us.

'You make the best cookies.'

I take another one and let it rest in my mouth. The sweet aroma of butter brings Sally back. When she died, I was only nine. For weeks afterwards, I kept sitting in front of her room, thinking that she'd come out and ask me to look at her monies.

The first time Sally let me into her room, was like being invited to enter a magic kingdom.

On the few rare occasions when Mum and Dad were away, the scent of cigarettes lingered in the corridor. When Sally opened the door, hazy patches of smoke snaked through the air.

'Wanna meet my new monies?' she asked.

Her room was like a secret chamber. I'd only ever caught a sneak peek before so, when she opened the door, I entered another world.

In Sally's room there were no peach walls with fairy stickers, like in mine. She'd stripped off the wallpaper and plastered the walls with posters and her drawings. A metal chandelier threw shadows onto her purple curtains.

Radiating with pride, Sally opened her sketchbook. A green dragon with red eyes stared back at me.

'Go ahead, you can touch him.'

'He is scary.'

'He just looks that way. Here, I'll show you.'

She traced her fingers over the dragon's head, all the way to the first flames that came out of its mouth.

'See? He's a friendly dragon.'

'But he spits fire.'

'That's because he needs to protect himself and his friends.'

I held Sally's hand and let her guide my fingers towards the paper. Its surface was smoother than it looked and felt pleasant under my fingertips.

'Would you like to have a dragon friend? He'll protect you, too, then.'

My hand hovered over the dragon's tail. For a moment there, I wanted to believe that Sally's monies could keep me safe.

'If you're his friend, you can visit him so he's not lonely,' Sally said.

'Do dragons get lonely?' I asked.

'Sometimes they do.'

Sally turned over the page in her sketchbook and showed me a purple and yellow monster. It had three feet and a long yellow tail that turned green and red at the end.

'This one,' Sally said, 'can make poison with a swipe of his tail.'

'Cannot!'

'Can, too.'

I pulled my hand away from the paper, which made Sally laugh. She lit a cigarette and let the smoke come out at the side of her mouth.

'He won't hurt you, silly.'

'You said he has poison.'

'Many things have poison. Like these,' she flicked the cigarette. 'Some plants and animals, too.'

'I don't like poison.'

'Dragon doesn't like it either, but his tail still makes it, so he can defend himself.'

'You can't just make poison.'

'Can, too.'

I shook my head. Sally put her arm around me. At that moment, it felt like we could take on the whole world, just Sally and me. If we had talked more, would she have said anything?

It was Dad who found Sally, hanging from a piece of rope tied around the chandelier in her room. By the time Mum and I got back from our hike, the ambulance had already put her on the bed. She was only sixteen, then. I remember her stripy pyjamas, her long, honey-coloured hair tied at the back, her lips darkened. Her green eyes bulged out, like the fish Dad sometimes brought from the market.

What a strange moment to decide to end your life. First thing in the morning, right after you wake up. Only a year later, I realised that Sally hadn't been sleeping that night. How could she have?

Dad found his own ways to cope with Sally's death. He collected all the rope he could find in the house and made a bonfire. Small strings in hoodies, old cables, wrapping ribbons, even Mum's knitting yarn. Mum just stared at the flames that licked the pyre, as though they could bring my sister back.

Mum stopped eating then, as if she, too, had decided it was time to go. Each night I crawled into her bed and wrapped my arms around her waist. I was afraid that if I let go, she would disappear, like Sally had. It took more than three weeks before she ate a full meal – a burnt chicken and oven-baked potatoes that Dad had made.

'You're a big girl now, Daphne,' Dad said. 'Why don't you leave Mum to get some rest?'

Having to sleep alone in my room felt like a punishment at the time, but Mum did get better. Soon, the whiff of sugar and spice brought our house back to life. Once again, there was lemon cake and rice pudding, but there would be no more butter cookies.

On Sundays, Mum made apricot pie.

'It's not my birthday, is it?' Dad asked, as he wolfed it down.

Mum smiled, kissed him on the cheek and put another big slice on his plate. He moaned from pleasure as he ate it. Back then, I thought that the worst was behind us. That as long as we were together, everything would be okay. I had no idea that Sally's death wasn't the end of the bad things. It was the beginning.

A rustle on the couch brings me back. Snowball yawns. For a brief moment, his cute little furry face stretches and distorts. He puts his long paws forwards before he curls up into a ball. If only I could do the same, just hide for a little while. Instead, I take one more piece of Christmas bread to feed the shadows. They only ever went away after Dad died but they never disappeared.

His death was unexpected, too. He dropped down after lunch, just like that. Heart attack, they said. Mum obsessively cleaned the house for a whole week, but wouldn't utter a word. When we walked home after the funeral, she squeezed my hand so tight that pain shot up to my eyes. I wanted to tell her, then. I was so close to telling her everything but when I opened my mouth, nothing came out. Even now, in my mind, the words resist surfacing.

I sink deeper into my armour and let the crunch of almonds in my mouth muzzle my stray thoughts. The only way to end this is to break the silence. I have to take Mum's hand and lead her to the edge of the gaping void and face what's inside. But Mum is all I have. Besides, what difference would it make? Sally is gone and so is Dad.

Mum lets the cupboard close with a bang. I twitch.

'I remember now,' she says. 'It's in the basement.'

'Mum, it's okay. There's no need—'

Before I can finish the sentence, she's already gone. Some minutes later, she's back with a small box full of jars.

'Take as many as you like, love.'

'Did you write down the recipe?' I ask.

She scratches her head.

'I did! But where is it?'

The same routine every year.

I take four pots filled with dark blue jelly and admire the handwriting on the label. It's neat and curvy, not a line out of place, as if it had been printed. Mum searches through piles of paper, her grey hair unruly and wild, her body restless.

'It's okay, Mum. Just sit down for a bit, will you?'

'It must be somewhere.'

'I'll just copy it from your notebook.'

Her eyes open wide as she glances at the battered green notebook on the shelf. Mum scratches her cheek.

'I'm not sure it's in this one.'

'Mum. You've always only had this one,' I say.

She twitches as I get up and puts her bony hand on mine. There's something in her eyes that makes me want to hug her, but I just stand there instead.

'Don't worry, Mum. I won't destroy anything.'

I kiss her hand and reach for the notebook. As I open it, Mum's arm jerks and knocks my teacup off the table. The brown liquid leaves a dark wet stain on the tablecloth and starts to trickle down. As I wipe it with a paper towel, I bump my foot against the sofa. Snowball gives me a disgruntled look.

The writing in the notebook is a bit faded, yet it's hard to miss the perfect loops around the l's and the beautifully curved a's and e's.

'I wish I could write like you, Mum.'

She chuckles nervously and leans forwards to see what I'm looking at. I find the recipe. Apricot jam.

'There it is. I guess it works for blueberries, too,' I say and start to copy it onto a piece of paper.

The thought of apricots twists my gut. The memory of Dad's moans, while he stuffed his face with pie, are just too much to stomach. He never said no when Mum offered another slice and would devour it as if it was the last piece of pie on Earth.

Mum's apricot craze didn't help. I was twelve, when for about three months, we were eating apricot everything. Cakes, pies, jams, sauces even. Every morning, a piece of pie would wait next to my dad's coffee. I still cannot stand the smell or taste of apricots. I thought that after so many weeks, Dad, too, would get bored. He never did.

Mum only stopped it after he died. I was relieved and not just because I didn't have to eat, see or smell another apricot ever again.

During the weeks after Dad's death, I lay awake on my bed and stared at the door, waiting for a release that never came. The doorknob didn't turn. It didn't wake me up and I didn't have to breathe in Dad's sweat on my skin. I was naive to think that I'd be free, that I'd ever be able to forget what he did to me, what he did to Sally.

Nothing could wash away the shame. Not standing under the hot shower until the skin on my fingers turned white and wrinkled. I sat on the bathroom floor, hugging my knees, letting the water beat against my skin. No amount of water made me feel clean enough or managed to wash away the vile taste in my mouth.

Our little secret, Dad called it, as though it was some broken vase. He said that no one would believe me. I believed him, then. Part of me still does.

Mum puts her hand on mine. Can she feel my discomfort? She looks at me and I think she's going to say something, but she just presses her lips together. Her eyes glisten with tears.

'Everything alright?'

'It's just a bit cold.'

She has always taken care of everything. I forget she, too, needs help.

'Let me make some tea,' I offer.

'You're a sweetheart.'

She snatches the green notebook from the table and puts it under her arm.

'Christmas movies are about to start,' she says. 'Want to watch?'

'You go ahead. I'll come when tea is ready.'

She leaves. Just as I am about to boil the water, I see a small piece of baking paper on the floor. It's folded together, much like a piece of chewing gum that's been wrapped so that it doesn't stick to an ashtray.

I want to toss it away but as I pick it up, I see something is written on it. I unfold it. There they are again, those perfect curves and lines. It takes me a while to grasp what I am looking at.

'It's starting!' Mum yells from the living room, trying to outdo the noise from the TV.

'I'll be there in a sec,' I say and straighten the piece of paper in my hand. My heart drums as I skim through the lines one more time.

160 apricot kernels

'See? I told you it's possible,' Sally said and tapped her finger on a newspaper clipping in her sketchbook. I leaned closer and tried to read it. My tongue almost crumbled as I read out the word printed in big fat letters.

'Cy-a-nide.'

'It was an accident, but you can see that I wasn't lying.'

'What kind of accident?' I asked.

'They ate parts they weren't supposed to eat,' Sally said.

'Fruit isn't poisonous,' I said.

'Some parts of it are, like apple pits or apricot kernels.'

'I can die if I eat them?'

Sally laughed.

'No, silly. You'd have to eat dozens and they don't taste that good.'

I found the whole idea ridiculous. Even if you could make cyanide, why would you? Besides, what would you do with all the apricots?

I fold the baking paper back and put it in my pocket. Next week, my friends are making a bonfire. They can always use more paper to get it started.

I push back the salty taste of tears. Maybe that void was a float all along.

'It's starting,' Mum says and chuckles.

'Coming!'

I give her a cup of tea and kiss her on the cheek. She hugs me. This time, I don't let go.

This story has been long-listed on Fish Publishing short story contest 2018/2019.

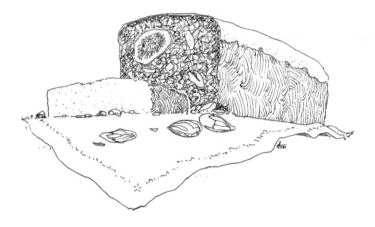

PASS THE KETCHUP

Hanneke checked her phone but there was still no message from her mother. She hadn't answered her 'Hey, did you see my new feature?' text, nor had she replied to Hanneke's email with the links to all the latest vloggers talking about how inspiring Hanneke's work was.

On the table below, a slice of avocado and coconut cake waited patiently. Hanneke repositioned the rustic tea towel and the copper spoon next to the plate, then climbed on a chair and sprinkled a handful of purple blossoms over the arrangement. She then moved a few blossoms and began taking photos.

The cake was sturdy enough to endure the photoshoot, unlike the mango and cashew one that had become a mushy mess of yellow and brown. After she'd taken photos from all possible angles, she checked them on her phone. She wouldn't want to miss an important detail. Her fans had used to love everything she published, but lately, there had been a few snarky comments.

How clean is this cake? Looks like you used white flour AND cream, LOL.

The plate's out of focus.

Looks EXACTLY like VW's detox smoothie with some decor.

Sure, her recipes weren't that different from Vegan Wendy's, but they were still hers. If her fans only knew how hard it was to come up with something completely original, something no one else had ever done, and make it delicious.

Hanneke paired the Bluetooth keyboard with her phone and typed: This fabulous coconut and avocado cake is proof that clean eating can accommodate a sweet tooth. It only has five ingredients. Click on my bio for the full recipe. #goodfood #cleandiet #cleanlife #glutenfree #vegan #healthylife #healthyfood #liveauthentic #Hannana

A moment after she'd published the photo, her phone started to buzz. Dozens of likes flooded in. Though her mother hadn't liked her last few photos, Hanneke hoped she'd at least seen them.

Hanneke made some herbal tea and, for the first time that morning, sat down to eat. The first bite was somewhat disappointing. She hoped that the addition of cashew nuts would make the cake taste better, but it still mostly tasted of avocado.

After the third spoonful, Hanneke binned the cake and opened the cupboard to look for something else to eat. There was hardly any other food left. She hadn't done her shopping for the week, but she also didn't feel like doing it. The last three days, she'd woken up with an inexplicable craving for chocolate chip cereal doused with honey. In her dreams, chocolate cake with whipped cream featured frequently, but not as frequently as pizza with anchovies, still sizzling from the oven.

Hanneke glanced at her reflection in a mirror. She was in better shape than ever. Her skin was firm and her muscles toned. Her fans told her that she glowed. She couldn't disagree. The only thing she was missing was the nice warm feeling in her belly, as though she'd been hugged from within.

Don't think about that.

The notion was already there, clinging to the edge of her thoughts. There was but one thing to do. Hanneke rushed to her desk and deployed her craving crusher, a folder with selected photos from her old life. She opened the one she hated most because her face was almost unrecognisable and coated in extra layers of skin and fat.

Want to go back to that?

She is grinning at the camera, unaware of the bits of olive pesto stuck between her teeth. In front of her is a plate with a large slice of pizza. Hanneke's gaze darted from the pizza to her double chin, then to the olive-stained teeth and the ketchup stain on her yellow dress and back to the pizza. Why hadn't her mother said something before snapping the photo? At least back then, her mother still came to her birthdays.

Hanneke's hair on the photo was a mess, but her eyes were strangely vibrant, like a pair of dark pearls. Closing the computer, she hopped onto her arc trainer. Physical exercise would help her get her mind off pizza. As she began the workout, new likes kept rolling in. At least her fans cared. What was her mother doing, anyway? She couldn't have been *that* busy.

Hanneke's thoughts galloped towards the frozen goods fridge in the local store. She hadn't been there in years but she could still remember most items with incredible clarity. There was ice cream, frozen fries and burgers, vegetables and ice-cream cakes and pizza.

Just one slice with double cheese and anchovies.

The thought implanted itself into Hanneke's mind. Who could help her? Not Irma, that's for sure. She'd loved Hannana before she turned vegan. Now, she couldn't stop glorifying Vegan Wendy, Hanneke's main rival. And as if this wasn't enough, Wendy was smart, gorgeous and more popular than anyone else.

No, Irma wouldn't be much help, nor would Quintain. He'd been very enthusiastic about Hanneke's food, when he was still new to clean eating and keen to suck up to the influencers. He'd been branching out, though, ignoring her posts and messages, just like her mother. It's always the quiet ones who slide a knife between your ribs.

Even a Margherita would do.

There was no way Hanneke could get a slice of pizza or

anything else that wasn't clean. It was only a matter of days before her fans would catch the rumours. After what had happened to Herb Paul, she knew how unforgiving they could be.

Yet, if she could sink her teeth into the crust, still warm and tinged with that intoxicating aroma of tomato sauce and cheese...

Hanneke closed her eyes and imagined holding a slice with the crust burnt from the oven. When she'd bite into it, the cheese would stretch like gum and fill her mouth with that unique taste of tomato, oregano and olive oil, a rapture on her tongue.

The image was so vivid in her head that she could almost smell the tomatoes and lick the salt off the anchovies. Saliva gathered in the back of her throat.

No one will find out. Promise.

Two streets away, there was a small shop where Hanneke used to buy snacks. She hadn't been there in years and she was pretty sure that none of her fans would want to be seen near such a place, either. It was perfect. She had to be careful, though. A light disguise would do the trick.

Hanneke went into the storage, a place where her fat clothes and old junk were sealed in boxes. It didn't take her too long to dig out her old jeans, now twice her size and stained with white paint. She'd need a belt to keep the pants from falling down but she didn't have one, so she took an old scarf and wrapped it around her waist. She pulled out a T-shirt from her 'giveaway' box, one with an image of a burger saying, 'Eat Me'. She'd got it as a present when they opened a new burger joint.

Hanneke changed and checked herself in the mirror. She tied her hair into a bun and stuffed it under a red baseball cap that said, 'Fire Brigade'.

She took one last look in the mirror, then donned her shades. No fans were waiting for her at the back door. She wasn't that sort of influencer yet but one could never be sure that someone wasn't hanging around, waiting for her to make an appearance. After the rift between some food bloggers, the yellow press was in need of embarrassing material.

The store had the same sad lighting Hanneke remembered. The once blue walls were now grey and covered in dust. Hanneke didn't bother taking a shopping trolley but she also couldn't simply walk up to the counter and demand a slice of pizza, so she grabbed a few caramel chocolate bars and stuck them in her pocket.

The store was practically empty, except for the couple who were fighting over what brand of beer to buy and the man with the moustache who was stocking up on kombucha. She'd been foolish to worry about anyone seeing her. Hanneke approached the pastry counter and locked her gaze onto a handsome slice of pizza. There were three left, one of them bigger than the others.

On the shelf below were tired-looking cinnamon rolls and very inviting-looking doughnuts with cream glaze. Her chest began to hammer.

A young woman appeared from the back and put down her sandwich.

'What can I get you?' she asked, with her mouth still full.

'I'll have that slice, please,' Hanneke said and pointed at the middle slice.

The woman didn't pay attention and reached for the slice closest to her.

'No,' Hanneke said. 'That one.'

The woman looked at Hanneke as if she was insane. Maybe to her, it didn't matter. It wasn't her only slice of pizza in over two years. There was at least half a centimetre more pizza on the middle slice. If she was allowed to have just one, it was going to be that one.

Reluctantly, the woman put the first slice back and took the one Hanneke was pointing at. She rolled her eyes as she put it onto a paper tray.

'Will that be all?' she asked.

'And these,' said Hanneke, taking the chocolate bars out of her pocket. The question seemed to be rhetorical as the woman was already busy microwaving her pizza slice. Heating the pizza would make it soggy but Hanneke didn't want to complain. She took the slip that registered the pizza and moved to the cashier's desk where a hip young man was scrolling down his phone. He glanced at the slip, then at Hanneke.

'Just the pizza?' he asked.

'Yes, and...'

Hanneke paused. What was she going to say again? The man looked at her for real, for the first time.

'Hey, don't I know you?' He stared at Hanneke's chin which made her uneasy.

'I don't think so.' Hanneke readjusted her shades. Could he see her eyes through them? Of course not. She was being silly.

Hanneke laid the banknotes on the counter. A foresight on her side, so no one could trace the purchase back to her card. She remembered about the chocolate, then.

'Oh, yeah,' she said and took the bars out of her pocket. 'I almost forget these.'

The man punched in the price and slid the bars back to Hanneke, who put them back into her pocket. He kept blinking at Hanneke's neck.

It was then that she remembered the necklace. Her back broke out in sweat. How could she have forgotten to take it off? The golden letter H stamped with a beehive pattern and laced with shiny stones was her logo. She went out of her way to promote it. She told everyone her mum had got her that necklace, though really, Hanneke had paid for it with her own money. Her hand flung towards her neck.

The woman brought a box with her pizza and placed it on the counter. The greasy stain on the box indicated the cheese was probably stuck to the top of the cardboard box, but this wasn't the time to fuss. The man and the woman exchanged a few hushed words. The woman glanced towards Hanneke, said something under her breath and went into a room in the back.

'I knew I'd seen you before,' the man said. 'You're that food blogger, aren't you? Hannana? My girlfriend is mad about your stuff.'

Hanneke shook her head furiously.

'That's not me, no.'

The man was pulling out his phone.

'Oh man, she'll die of envy when she sees the photo,' he said. 'She'll just die.'

Hanneke's throat knotted. Before she could put up her hand and hide her face, the guy snapped a photo of her, an unflattering one at that. Her fans wouldn't recognise her but they'd know the necklace.

'One more,' said the guy and turned, so he was closer to Hanneke.

'Stop,' said Hanneke. 'No more photos.'

The man paused then chuckled, as though she'd said something funny, and snapped a few more. Heat gushed into Hanneke's cheeks. Fuck the pizza. She grabbed the cash and ran for the exit.

'Come on, man! Why are you such a bitch?'

Hanneke heard footsteps but she didn't stop to check.

'Did she nick those chocolates?' someone in the back asked.

'We can check,' someone else said. 'I've filmed it.'

Hanneke's chest hammered. The sun was high and seemed to have bleached the world of visual pleasure. Running would draw attention, so she walked with brisk steps instead. Her jeans were sliding down her hips. Though she kept pulling them up, she wasn't sure how long they would last.

She couldn't go straight home because that would confirm who she was. Later, she could always make up a story about a twin necklace. As she power-walked, she kept checking the reflection in her phone. A few people were following her. At least they seemed to be walking at the same pace. Two of them had their phones up and looked like they were filming.

Hanneke pulled the baseball hat down over her eyes and

picked up the pace. She almost knocked down a bunch of teenagers that were hanging out on the street.

'Look! It's Hannana!'

A few shrieks and more shuffling of feet behind her. More people were filming, too. Hanneke was sure of it.

Bile started to rise in her stomach. She tucked the necklace under her T-shirt.

'Hey, Hannana!' someone shouted behind her. 'Stop acting like a fucking bitch!'

'Did you really nick the pizza?' someone else yelled.

'Yeah, your fans want to know!'

Hanneke's phone buzzed. She pushed it deeper into her pocket and ran towards the city market. Once inside, she mixed with the crowd, dropped her baseball hat into a bin and rolled the sleeves of her T-shirt to the inside. One of the shops sold cheap clothes. She grabbed an ugly T-shirt and a pair of cheap sunglasses.

'Keep the change.' She handed the woman a twenty.

'It's thirty-five,' said the woman.

Hanneke paid and asked, 'Where's the changing room?'

'We don't have one,' the woman said. 'Try there.' She pointed at the bar across the aisle.

Dots flickered in front of Hanneke's eyes. She put on her new sunglasses and walked into the bar. It was a hipster bar that resembled a warehouse, except for the flashy food display and the counter. Though Hanneke only glimpsed at the cakes there, they looked exactly like the ones she'd been dreaming about.

Not clean, just tasty.

She locked herself in the bathroom and checked her phone. Over seven hundred notifications and two missed calls: one from Vegan Wendy, the other one from her mum. Hanneke's stomach felt like an oddly shaped rock, tumbling around.

She checked Vegan Wendy's message first.

'Congrats on going viral! Coming for an autograph ;).'

Below the message were two links. The first one was to a

YouTube video. It couldn't be good news, not if Wendy had sent it.

Hanneke's knees went wobbly when she saw the title: Hannana robs a local store. The shaky video showed Hanneke trying to avoid being filmed. The second link was a mash-up clip of Hanneke raising her hand and the man behind the counter saying, 'Why are you such a bitch?' The video and the man's voice were looped against headache-inducing music. Every time she put her hand up, her logo flashed on the screen.

She exhaled loudly. It wasn't as bad as she'd thought. At least no one had mentioned the pizza. Coming up with a plausible explanation shouldn't be too difficult. Then, the camera zoomed in to her necklace before the footage went black. It must have been the pizza woman filming from the back room.

The video had thousands of views. Hanneke vomited the dark green mash of her avocado cake, the only thing she'd eaten that day, then dry-heaved over the toilet. Her brain felt as if it was going to split her head open.

When it became clear nothing more would come out of her stomach, Hanneke sat down and checked the second message. Her mum didn't care for social media. She couldn't have known anything.

The message was short.

'What the heck are you wearing? I wired some money. X'

Below the message was a link to an Instagram story of Hanneke ordering a pizza, followed by Hanneke taking the money and rushing out of the store. The camera zoomed in on her butt, most of which was covered by jeans, except for the upper rim of her underpants. It was white, for Christ's sake. The XL was visible on the tag of her jeans that had flipped out.

Hanneke hid her face between her palms. This was it, then, the fall of Hannana, a star blogger and the clean food advocate. From now on, shame and misery would drip into her life. There'd be no more interviews, no more blogger conferences. Even if she continued to publish videos and make new recipes, people wouldn't trust her. They'd flock to Vegan Wendy. They were flocking already. Their comments would get meaner and meaner till she'd have to take it all offline.

Hanneke rubbed her eyes and felt tiny bits of mascara crumble under her fingertips. Let it get smudged. Who cares, anyway? Not the people filming her. Clearly not her own mother.

So what if there were no more presents and freebies? The only thing she'd miss were messages from her fans about how inspiring she was and what a difference she made in their lives. They wouldn't have said those things if they didn't care about her.

Hanneke wiped away the tears with the back of her palm. Maybe her fans would defend her, maybe they'd come up with an explanation, say it was all a test, a celebrity stunt by their favourite food blogger. Holding her breath, Hanneke glanced at the comments underneath the video.

Busted!

What a disaster, LOL!

Unfollow!

Wtf is she wearing? Did she rob a tramp?

I told you she was a fake! Live Authentic, my ass!

Hanneke blew her nose into the toilet paper. No one had come to defend her; no one cared. The most generous comment among the first dozen was 'Well, shit happens'. She wasn't going to read the rest.

She'd been there before. Being unwanted was familiar What did it matter in the end? She'd had a few good years. Her life wasn't over. These days, many things could be fixed with the help of a delete button. Then, it would be as though Hannana had never existed.

In her settings, she pressed 'delete account'. No more Instagram. She didn't need YouTube, either. No account meant no tagging and no notifications. Delete! Next, she went into her Facebook account. Her fingers trembled for a few seconds, then she deleted everything. Her chest felt lighter.

So what if she got no more invites or discounts? Most of them were lame things she never used anyway. She definitely wouldn't miss avocado cakes, nor grilled cabbage canapés with fresh mint. In fact, she'd never have to eat cabbage again.

Her eyes widened.

Pizza.

She'd have a big fucking slice. Forget a slice, she'd have the whole damned thing.

She smiled. Yes, she thought, that's exactly what I'll do. She'd book a table at her old favourite pizza place and invite her mother to join. Pizza was the one thing her mother couldn't say no to.

Hanneke opened the bathroom and washed her hands. Then, she removed the few bits of smudged mascara from her face and released the bun, so her hair fell over her shoulders.

Her eyes were red and puffy but they glowed, just like on that photo from her birthday.

When Hanneke came out of the toilet, a few people were loitering around the bar area holding their phones, their fingers ready to record. Hanneke walked to the bar and scanned the blackboard with the specials. She wouldn't go back home hungry, especially not as she had hardly any food in her fridge.

The waiter wiped the counter and leaned forward to display a tattoo of a monstera leaf on his arm.

'What can I get you?' he asked.

'A cappuccino,' Hanneke said and laid some crumpled banknotes on the counter. 'Do you have anything like a pizza?'

'Umm, yes, we have a focaccia.'

'I'll have one, thank you,' Hanneke said.

A few gasps escaped as she turned to one of the cameras. So, Vegan Wendy really had come to gloat.

'Hey, Wendy,' Hanneke outstretched her hand. 'Could you please pass the ketchup?'

LET IT ROT

Most of her old trousers and skirts rounded weirdly around the bump that was now her stomach. Since her son had been born, she'd been drooled over, vomited on and covered in spit. Not tonight, though. The new blue dress made her feel pretty. She combed her hair and put on her cherry lipstick. Still, whenever she passed a mirror, her eyes drew invisible lines around her hips, her extruded belly and her breasts.

Smaller portions, a little less wine.

Once she got rid of the stubborn fat, her husband would pull her close again and kiss her neck, as he used to.

She waited for him to get home, then wrapped her hands around his neck and kissed him. He put his hand around her waist and pinched her.

'Saving for hard times, are you?' he said.

No more wine, sweets and cereal bars.

He put down his briefcase.

'I'll change before dinner,' he said.

She glanced at the calendar to make sure she hadn't mixed up the dates.

'Aren't we eating out?'

His forehead wrinkled, then his eyes gravitated towards the circled date on the calendar.

'Oh,' he said. 'Yes, we are.'

It was the first time he'd forgotten about their wedding anniversary but she didn't hold it against him.

'I've booked our usual place,' she said.

'What if we tried something new?'

'Like what?'

'There's this new hip place just a bit out of town,' he said. 'My colleagues think it's worth checking out.'

She sucked in her stomach and put on a smile.

'Sounds great.'

As they drove to the restaurant, she worried about whether she'd given the babysitter all the information, then composed a list of things she'd allow herself to eat. A salad, she thought, with a small steak or a piece of fish, grilled, not fried. Maybe a cookie, if it came with the coffee, but she wouldn't order a dessert.

The restaurant smelled of fried food and beer. Her husband ordered pasta carbonara and a bottle of the cheapest red wine on the menu. When the waiter wanted to pour some in her glass, she shook her head.

'Just sparkling water, please.'

Her salad tasted like wet grass and the steak was rubbery. She pushed the food around her plate. Her husband arched his eyebrows.

'What's the matter?'

'It's too much.'

'You've only had a few bites.'

'I'm already full.'

He paused, as if thinking.

'Maybe you're a breatharian,' he said after a few moments.

'A what?'

'People who eat air or energy or something.'

'That's impossible.'

'It's very possible,' he said. 'I read about this woman who feeds on sunlight. How cool is that?'

She didn't want to put him in a bad mood, so she nodded.

'Could be,' she said.

'You should try it,' he said. 'If it turns out I'm right, and I think I am, it'd be amazing.'

'How so?'

'Do you know how rare that is? To have such a skill?'

Her husband eyed her plate. She pushed it over to his side and ordered coffee. There was no biscuit with it, only a wrapped, coffee-flavoured hard candy.

'You really think this air eating works?'

'It'd be very practical,' he said, 'and we'd save money.'

When they got back home, their son woke up and started to cry.

'Would you mind taking care of that?' he asked. 'I've got some work to finish.'

He said this as though it wasn't his child, too. She lay on her son's bed and sang to him till he fell asleep. Listening to his gentle breathing calmed her down. Before she drifted away, she thought about eating light. It sounded wrong, yet interesting at the same time. She decided to look into it.

Eating light only worked for half of the day, when she was too busy to realise she was hungry. As soon as her son took his first nap, her stomach began to roar. Since she'd already announced her new diet to her husband, she couldn't eat anything from the fridge. He'd notice. She went into the basement instead and inspected the roots and vegetables they kept there.

Which of those was most like air? Not carrots, for sure. They were sweet and delicious. Beetroot was too tricky and would stain her fingers. The last box contained some pale green roots. She'd bought them at a discount and planned to make them into a soup. She sniffed them and detected no scent. When she peeled one of them, the inside was white and watery-looking. The taste was mild, almost non-existent. This, she decided, was perfect and the closest to air there was. Her husband only went into the basement if she asked him to fix something. Most of the time, he'd forget anyway.

In the following weeks, she read more about breatharianism and stacked the basement shelves with kohlrabi, from pickled to sweet and fresh. The new diet had an almost immediate effect, albeit it left her with a permanent feeling of hunger.

'The air feeding really suits you,' he said.

'Do you think so?'

'Wait till my colleagues find out about this. They're going to be so jealous.'

'Oh, I'm not sure. Maybe it's best not to tell anyone, in case it doesn't work out.'

'You should be proud. A wife who feeds on air? Now, there's a headline for you.'

She smiled, because she liked the way he looked at her and the way he kissed her every time he got home. Luckily, the basement door locked automatically, but she could sneak in whenever she needed a bite. Kohlrabi wasn't enough, though, and she found inventive ways to eat in secret. Her body started to feel firm again and her newest clothes too loose. When she could, she sneaked out and bought real food in places where no one knew her, but with her husband, she only drank water.

'We need to celebrate,' he said.

'There's no need, really.'

'There sure is. People could learn from you.'

Despite her reluctance, he booked a table at their favourite restaurant. She ate beforehand, but she still found it hard to watch her husband gobble down a whole pizza.

'Dessert?' the waiter asked.

'Not for her.' Her husband took the dessert menu. 'She feeds on air.'

The waiter's smile froze, as though he didn't react at all.

'You don't have to tell everyone,' she said.

'Why the hell not?'

If her husband went on like this, she'd never be able to get out of this diet. That night, he pinched her bottom as he helped her into a cab. His hands were all over her, almost as if there were four and not just two. When they got home, he devoured her, much like the pizza earlier.

Such nights became more frequent. Every time she thought about telling him she wanted to quit, she thought about the things she could lose, like how he talked about her and how he lingered in the morning before leaving for work.

A few months later, her breasts started to round and soften. They'd talked about having another child. She missed kissing the puffy baby's head and inhaling the milky scent, but her husband was convinced it was too soon.

That night, she sat her husband down and prepared a meal: mashed potatoes, salad and some grilled kohlrabi. He frowned at the sight of two empty plates at the table.

'Who's the other one for?' he asked.

'Our new baby.'

The husband reached for the potatoes. 'What if he can feed on light?'

'He can't, okay?'

She helped herself to some grilled kohlrabi. He eyed it with disgust.

'What the hell is that thing?'

'Some vitamins,' she said and loaded her plate. It was a relief not to have to hide anymore, so she took a big portion and savoured each bite.

'Why do you say 'he'?' she added. 'Might be a baby girl.'

He didn't seem too impressed with the idea and she didn't particularly want to discuss it any further. He'd have time to adapt to it, no doubt. She wasn't certain he'd adapt to the idea of eating kohlrabi, though. He didn't touch a single piece and didn't come to bed until late.

Ever since her son had gone to day care, she'd begun to notice things. How her husband took his phone to the bathroom even when he showered and how he often came out chuckling while looking at it. He fell asleep before she came to bed and in the morning, he just grabbed his coffee and rushed off. It was almost as if eating with her disgusted him. As if *she* disgusted him.

There was not much time to ponder, though, with this new life to take care of. She'd still venture into the basement for the occasional snack. Being in a cool place helped her straighten her thoughts. She made kohlrabi on a few more occasions, hoping her husband would change his mind. Once fried, then sauteed and finally marinated. He never touched it.

'Take this away,' he said.

'At least give it a try.'

'If you want to eat *that*, I won't stop you,' he said, 'but don't put it on my plate ever again.'

The next time she went into the basement, the stairs felt a bit wobbly. There was a crack in the water pipe and a few loose tiles needed readjusting. Before she could ask her husband to fix anything, she'd have to hide her secret stash of snacks, not to mention the kohlrabi. Since he refused to eat any, a few roots had rotted. They gave out an acrid scent, as though something had died in there.

When her belly became very rounded, her husband got into the habit of pinching the extra flesh under her chin.

'Might be good to start that air diet again,' he said.

It might be good if you stopped talking.

Out of spite, she bought a few more kilos of kohlrabi and stocked it on the shelves.

Let it rot.

Occasionally, she hid kohlrabi in soup and potato puree. Her husband paused as he chewed, but he couldn't quite tell what was different. How could he, when he'd never tasted it?

When he was away for work, she cooked all her favourite dishes, like oven-baked pancakes and courgette strudel. She froze the leftovers and snacked on them when he wasn't home.

Because of her belly, she needed support when she climbed the stairs. The banister was wobbly, too, like many other things in the basement, and the stairs sighed like planks on a suspension bridge. One of the nails had come out. She made a mental note to tell her husband.

The next day, she gave him a list of things that needed fixing. He murmured something about 'checking that later' and left for work. Nothing happened for two more weeks. When her delivery of groceries arrived, she emptied the bag with tins onto the stairs and watched them tumble down. A few got stuck on the way. The top of one of the steps looked as if it was coming off, but whenever she brought it up, her husband muttered under his breath and announced he had work to do.

Shortly before their daughter was born, she overheard him comparing her to an animal. It wasn't a cuddly animal either, rather a farm animal, bred for slaughter. That day, she sneaked into the cellar and kicked the tins around on the stairs. She climbed down a few steps, propping herself up against the wobbly banister, and kicked the broken plank away. Then, she sat down and cried for a while.

After their daughter was born, he started to come home late again. Sometimes, he'd come to bed in the middle of the night and stink of smoke and sweat.

'You're hardly ever home,' she told him in the morning as she cradled their baby daughter.

Their son was bashing his spoon into the cereal bowl, spilling milk all over the table.

'We need the money,' he said. 'Unless you want to skip the holidays.'

'Holidays? Where to?' she asked.

'It'd have to be short,' he said, 'and not too far away, in case something urgent comes up at work.'

'Surely, we can manage two weeks somewhere? I don't mind if it's close. We could maybe go to the coast?'

'For God's sake.' Her husband pulled the spoon out of his son's hands.

The boy's face froze, then he started to cry.

'I can take a week, max,' her husband said. 'Can't take more than that. There's too much work.'

'We could rent a flat,' she said. 'Save some money. I could cook for us.'

'That doesn't sound like a good idea,' he said, smoothing his tie. 'If you want something longer, though, you could visit your mother, stay with her the week before.'

'Alone?'

'With the kids, obviously. I can't take care of them with all the work.'

He grabbed his briefcase and headed for the door.

'Don't forget to fix the basement stuff,' she shouted.

He raised his hand and left.

She saved pockets of time to plan the holiday. Her mother was happy to welcome her and the kids. She needed to fetch a few things from the basement but she wasn't too keen on going down there, so she postponed it until the week before the holidays.

She'd hardly made it to the middle of the steps, careful not to step on any of the tins, when the lightbulb buzzed and went dark.

Just as well. He has to fix it, anyway.

Slowly, she turned, waiting for her eyes to adjust to the dark before making a move. With careful steps, she moved up and was almost at the top when the key turned. She heard her husband's voice speaking in a hushed tone. She wouldn't have heard him if he hadn't been standing right in front of the basement door.

'This Friday,' he said. 'The whole week, yeah.'

Something behind her eyes tensed. It wasn't the flat voice he used with his colleagues.

'Don't forget condoms,' he said. 'I don't have any.'

His words smouldered in her belly like charcoal. She struggled to breathe. When her husband went upstairs to change, she sneaked out and pretended to have come from the shop.

The first thing she did was order ten kilos of kohlrabi. That evening, she made a stew and served it for dinner. Her husband frowned.

'I told you I didn't want to touch that shit ever again,' he said.

'Don't eat it then.'

He pushed the plate away, ordered pizza and ate it in front of the TV.

She threw the rest of kohlrabi down the stairs and pushed the door till it locked with a click.

He'll have to touch it, now.

On the morning of their departure, she got up early to get the kids ready. Every time she passed the basement door, she sniffed at the air to confirm the odour had become more pungent. There were a few rotten pieces there already and the new ones would rot soon enough.

'Ready to go?' her husband asked.

'I couldn't get the pool stuff,' she said. 'It's still in the basement.'

His cheeks tightened.

'I'll fix the stuff, okay. I said I would.'

'I need it now, though, don't I?'

Her husband glanced at his wristwatch.

'The kids will be cranky if they can't use the pool,' she said, holding her daughter, 'and mum can't exactly hide it.'

'Fine. Where in the basement?'

'Where we keep the garden stuff.' She moved her daughter to her other arm. 'All the way in the back.'

His steps were heavy as he approached the basement. She waited for the bang when the open door slammed against the wall.

'Stinks like shit in here,' he said.

'Hold your breath,' she said, taking her son's hand.

The door locked with a click.

'Fuck! The light is out!'

'Wait a second,' she said. 'Your eyes will adjust.'

'Fuck this shit, I'm not doing it.'

'Won't take a minute,' she said.

'Open the door.'

'Let me put the kids in the car first. I don't want them running around. I left a torch on the stairs.'

'Where?'

'In the middle.'

There was a crack of breaking wood, then a loud thump, followed by tumbling and muffled cries of pain. She took the kids to the front door. Outside, the sun was shining. Her neighbours waved at her as they passed by with their poodle.

She turned back into the house.

'I'll miss you too,' she shouted. 'Don't forget your swimsuit. See you in a week!'

After she'd locked the front door, she secured the kids into the car. Then she started the engine and whistled all along the way.

THE COLLECTORS

From:Theodor.windman@vub.ac.be
To:Gregory.Mason@vub.ac.be
Date: 20 May 2018, 14:10

Gregster!

I made it to Austria. Loved the schnitzel btw! Thanks for the tip. I would have fallen straight into a food coma if it weren't for the schnapps.

The locals are friendly, but not very helpful. No one seemed to understand what I was saying. Some grandma was even shaking her head. She probably thought I was gonna climb the mountains in flip flops or something.

Bad news about the second half of that Alex Schmidt article: I googled like crazy but didn't find it. Nor Alex Schmidt, for that matter. Let's hope he didn't have the same idea as us, so we can claim all the fame & glory.

How's your leg btw? I still can't believe you're missing this (schnitzel, man!) No more vodka jelly shots for you. Maybe you're just getting old ;)

Not sure how much signal there will be up there but I'll drop you a line when I'm back in town. Shouldn't take more than a few days. Fingers crossed!

Cheers,

Theo

From:Gregory.Mason@vub.ac.be
To:Theodor.windman@vub.ac.be
Date: 20 May 2018, 18:23

Nerdo,

Me and my leg are fine. The cast is actually quite handy when you need somewhere to rest an ashtray or hang a coat or if you're looking for an excuse to get out of washing dishes.

Can't believe you were knocked down by a schnitzel! You'd starve in the wild, LOL. Don't even try something more hardcore, like a knödel. It's a bread dumpling that might kill you.

Fuck Alex Schmidt! I was really hoping you'd get further with that article than me (seriously – only a paper version in this day & age?). You wouldn't believe the shit our librarian gave me for not reporting 'vandalism', as she called it. As if I was the one who'd torn half of it out and then sent a virus to their archive.

Why would they order only one copy, anyway? I hope whoever took it isn't doing research about Neolithic mass graves or skeletons without broken shinbones.

Take it easy on that schnapps, Nerdo. You know you can't handle liquor and I don't want to have to fundraise to get your skinny ass back home. We'll have a proper pub crawl when you're back.

I know you'll be off the grid, but I'll be sending some useful stuff I found today. For starters, I've added a few sentences to our research proposal – see what you think:

All the evidence found in Neolithic mass graves demonstrates ancient beliefs in life beyond death. In killings to acquire territory, the soldiers would break the shins of their victims in order to prevent them from returning as ghosts. However, recent excavations in Germany and Austria prove not all dead bodies had broken shins. We can therefore assume this belief was not widely shared.

Break a leg ;)

Greg

P.S. Your mum called again. Maybe let her know you're alive? While you're at it, try to get her to send more of that salami. Think of your poor flatmate with the broken leg.

<attachment: Anthropology of Death, research methodology.pdf>

∼

From:Theodor.windman@vub.ac.be
To:Gregory.Mason@vub.ac.be
Date: 21 May 2018, 07:04

Finally, I got some signal. Only took me half an hour of walking around in the middle of nowhere. Rock and grass and grass and rock. Feels almost as if I'm on another planet.

Speaking of which, you should have seen the locals I'm crashing with. Chris and Sandra would look great on the cover of Stephen King's *Misery*. She has that bewildered Kathy Bates look and cuts her own hair, and he's always scribbling something. She's also obsessed with cooking. Not sure how much more I can eat, but I guess I'll find out.

Chris knows some guy who dug out bones a while ago (not as a hobby, I hope). I'll stick around to see if he knows anything. I've tried to bring up the ghost village story but all Chris and Sandra want to talk about is food. Maybe I have to get them drunk (we did say we wanted fresh and creative methodology, right?).

If I don't get anywhere in the next two days, I'll go back. Tomorrow, Sandra is making her famous soup. She goes on and on about it, some kind of national dish or something. No knödel in it, I checked.

Thanks for the stuff you sent. I'll take a closer look when I get back to civilisation.

Cheers,

Theo

<attachment: location Theo Windman.jpg>

From:Gregory.Mason@vub.ac.be
To:Theodor.windman@vub.ac.be
Date: 22 May 2018, 14:08

Smells like a Fulbright scholarship (unless that Sandra woman plans to keep you and feed you till you become a sumo fighter).

If you do find that bone guy, go by the book and leave the digging to the pros. You wouldn't want to mess up the material by accident.

The map you sent makes no sense. There's nothing there: the closest village is like an hour's hike away. Sure your GPS wasn't off?

Btw, I finally got news about Alex Schmidt (and I now get why we couldn't find him). It's not a him, it's a her. Can you believe it? Alex is short for Alexandra. No one knows where she went after her Erasmus.

Keep me posted,

Greg

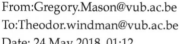

From:Gregory.Mason@vub.ac.be
To:Theodor.windman@vub.ac.be
Date: 24 May 2018, 01:12

Theo,

Everything OK up there? Tried to call you but it says your number can't be reached. Did you forget to pay the bill again?

Lucky you! I'd love to have someone to cook for me, too. I guess you've headed back already. Have fun with your locals and let me know when you're at the airport (and call your mum – she called three times today!).

See you in four days. Don't miss your flight!
Greg

∾

From:Fiona.Windman@gmail.com
To:Gregory.Mason@vub.ac.be
Date: 27 May 2018, 14:05

Dear Gregory,

I tried calling you today but you were busy. Any news from our Theodor? He was supposed to come home but we haven't heard anything from him. Did he mention visiting any friends? I can't get him on the phone. I am, quite frankly, beside myself. He's never disappeared like this before.

His bill has been paid now (thanks for the scan). I've called the police. If you hear from him, please call me immediately on +44 797 130019.

Regards,
Fiona

∾

From:Gregory.Mason@vub.ac.be
To:Fiona.Windman@gmail.com
Date: 27 May 2018, 19:37

Dear Mrs Windman,

I'm sorry I've missed your calls –I forgot my phone in the office. As said, I haven't heard from Theo since 21 May. He was still in the Austrian mountains and was doing well. I attach the map he sent.

He didn't mention seeing friends. It could be that he found something useful for our research and decided to stay longer. The signal in the mountains is usually quite bad.

He had been staying with two people called Sandra and Chris (in case it helps).

Tomorrow, we have a meeting with our mentor, so I hope to see him there. There's a chance he'll fly in and come directly there. I'll call you the minute I know more. I'll talk to the police today.

Best regards,

Greg

<attachment: location Theo Windman.jpg>

From:Gregory.Mason@vub.ac.be
To:SOS_rescue@bergen.at
Cc:Fiona.Windman@gmail.com, Theodor.windman@vub.ac.be
Date: 28 May 2018, 13:02

Dear Sir/Madam,

My friend, Theodor Windman went missing in the Austrian mountains on 21 May 2018.

He's 27, about 180 cm tall, skinny and has short brown hair and green eyes (recent photo attached). He was most likely wearing mountain shoes, a dark blue winter jacket and a grey hat. He's a British citizen, studying in Brussels.

His trip was part of our academic research on Neolithic mass graves. His plan was to visit several places to collect the data.

The last time I heard from him, he was staying with two locals (Sandra & Chris – see attached his last location).

His return ticket was never used and neither I, nor his mother (in cc), were able to reach him. The police have been informed and are in touch with Austrian authorities.

Thank you for any information you have.

Best regards,

Gregory Mason

<attachment: location Theo Windman.jpg>
    <attachment: Theo Windman photo.jpg>

~

From: SOS_rescue@bergen.at
To:Gregory.Mason@vub.ac.be
Cc:Fiona.Windman@gmail.com, Theodor.windman@vub.ac.be
Date: 29 May 2018, 10:41

Herr Mason,

Thank you for your email. Unfortunately, we haven't been able to locate Theodor Windman or get any information on his whereabouts.

The location you sent us hasn't been inhabited for the past 50 years. Even though three old cottages still exist in the area, no one lives there.

However, there is a similar case in our database dating back seven years: a journalist went missing at more or less exactly the same location. His name is Christopher Stieglitz.

His wife requested to be informed in case of similar events, as she might be able to help. With her consent, I enclose her contact details (MariaStieglitz@reflext.at), should you want to get in touch for more information.

We will inform you of any developments.

Mit freundlichen Grüßen,
Heinrich Puller
SOS rescue Austria

∼

From:Gregory.Mason@vub.ac.be
To:Fiona.Windman@gmail.com
Date: 31 May 2018, 21:45

Dear Mrs Windman,

I'm sorry for not answering your calls. I need to see what I can find out about Theo, so this morning I flew to Vienna.

Please don't worry about me. My leg is much better and I've been to Austria before. Tomorrow morning I'll head into the mountains. There is a cable car that can get me to the mountain from the village where Theo was last seen.

I also wrote to a woman named Maria Stieglitz and sent her all the information we have. I hope she can help us find Theo.

I hope to return with good news.

Best regards,

Greg

∼

From:MariaStieglitz@reflext.at
To:Gregory.Mason@vub.ac.be
Cc: Fiona.Windman@gmail.com
Date: 2 June 2018, 15:06

Dear Gregory,

Thank you for your kind email.

As you know, my husband, Chris, disappeared in the mountains while doing research for his book about local folklore. He was especially interested in folk tales about a ghost village. He never finished it.

Chris was in contact with the archaeological institute about evidence on bodies without broken shins. I used to think that his theory about murdered villagers' ghosts seeking revenge was just a tale. I do not think that anymore.

About five years ago, another student got in touch with me, also from Brussels. She was very keen to get there first and wouldn't wait a few days for a local mountaineer. She lost her phone at exactly the same location where my Chris and your friend were last seen. Her name was Alexandra (Sandra) Schmidt. It might be worth getting in touch with her.

I understand you're concerned about your friend's disappearance. However tempted you are to go and search for him, please do not go on your own! In the past 50 years, around a dozen people have gone missing there. According to folklore, the ghosts of murdered villagers can only avenge their deaths by collecting souls and increasing the number of ghosts.

If you decide to go against my advice, please do not eat anything once you're up in the mountains. After going through my husband's findings, I have reason to suspect that those who disappeared were poisoned.

I wish you all the best,

Maria

This story has been first published in 2019, in The Circle 19: a Brussels Anthology by Idle Time Press.

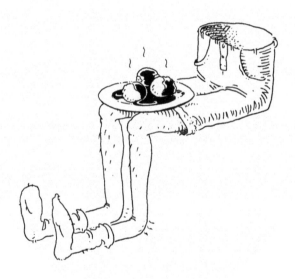

BE MY GUEST

Apéritif

Larissa double-checked the house number before ringing the doorbell. Turning up on the wrong doorstep would be a stupid mistake, given the size of the neighbourhood.

The footsteps on the other side of the door came closer. The light on the veranda went on. The door opened.

'Great, you've made it,' Bernadette said. To Larissa, she was the baguette lady who came every morning around ten to buy her baguette and chat about the weather. It had occurred to Larissa that Bernadette wasn't actually coming for the baguette. She had a way with people that made it so easy to tell her things they didn't plan to.

Larissa couldn't explain why she'd told Bernadette about her fiancé, but she had. Bernadette put on a sad face and told her she was sorry, then invited her over for dinner. How could she have said no?

She handed Bernadette a chilled bottle of Pinot Grigio but held onto the box that contained the cake. Her staff had been clear that the cake wouldn't survive much shuffling around and that unless

Larissa wanted to serve a chocolate mess, she'd have to keep it in a fridge.

When Bernadette pointed at the cake, Larissa said, 'Can I put it in the fridge?'

'You didn't have to bring it here.'

Bernadette showed Larissa in.

'Wasn't I supposed to bring dessert?'

'Not bring, no, but it's alright. It's your first time.'

Larissa tried to remember what Bernadette had said to her about the dinner. She'd definitely mentioned neighbours and something about being progressive. Had she said progressive dinner? That sounded plain silly. What would such a dinner even look like? Would they be talking about politicians screwing things up?

Progressive or not, Larissa was sure of one thing. Bernadette had said she had to take care of dessert.

The living room looked as if it had been decorated in the previous century. Green brocade curtains were covered in hideous golden flowers that reminded Larissa of crumpled tissue. The old oak furniture with brass handles fit very well with the landscape and still-life paintings with dead ducks.

Bernadette put the Pinot Grigio in the fridge and took out a jar of olives. She tipped a few onto a plate and gestured to Larissa to come closer.

'There.' Bernadette pointed at the half-empty shelf.

'Looks as if I'm the first one,' Larissa said and put the cake in the fridge.

'It's not a particularly punctual bunch,' Bernadette said.

She took out a bottle of wine that was no longer full, unscrewed the top and leaned over the bottleneck, as if she was trying to smell if it had gone bad. She poured two glasses.

'I love to start with some Chianti.' She handed Larissa a glass.

The sour tinge tugged at Larissa's cheeks. She'd only ever used Chianti in cooking.

Bernadette sat in an armchair, so Larissa sat down on the sofa across from her.

'So, Lara,' Bernadette said.

'Larissa.'

'Have you gotten used to living here?'

'It's very peaceful,' Larissa said.

She thought about what else to say, but the words that came to her mind were boring, small-minded and nosy, so she said nothing.

'It's great to see Noonan's Delights in capable hands,' Bernadette said.

'Oh, you're too kind,' Larissa said and meant it.

What did she know about running the bakery? She'd only taken it because it was a good deal that came with extra money and a discount on the house. It was the best offer she'd got. With the love of her life snapped away from her, what other choice did she have?

'How are you getting on with the staff?' Bernadette asked.

'They're lovely.' Larissa took a sip of wine. They *were* lovely when they weren't bickering or complaining, which wasn't very often.

The sound of the doorbell made Bernadette leap from her armchair. As she headed towards the door, Larissa spotted a tear in her turquoise Chanel tunic.

'Eddie!' Bernadette kissed the air around the man's cheeks. 'Lara is already here.'

'It's Larissa,' Larissa said, then quickly decided that Lara was alright.

Maybe it was better if they didn't know her real name. It would be like an extra layer of skin to protect her from the truth.

'Glad to finally meet you.' Eddie shook Larissa's hand.

His palm was soft and clammy. He looked like someone who'd got beaten up a lot in school.

'Where's Becca?' Bernadette asked.

Eddie sighed. 'Another conference. You know how it is with these things. She'll take any chance she gets.'

'That woman works too hard,' Bernadette said, and went to the kitchen.

'You tell her that.' Eddie sat down on the other end of the couch. 'She won't listen to me.'

He bit into an olive. A hint of surprise painted across his face, followed by a slight frown. Larissa tried an olive. It was salty and tasted like a dead oyster. She spit the olive into a napkin and crumpled it up in her hand. Eddie did the same.

Bernadette returned from the kitchen with a glass of wine for Eddie and a bag of cashew nuts. She tossed them on the table.

'How's the bakery?' Eddie asked.

'Busy,' Larissa said.

'That won't change, if you're lucky,' Eddie said.

'I don't know about that,' Larissa said.

'Did Lara tell you about her husband?' Bernadette asked.

'Fiancé,' Larissa said.

'No, she didn't.'

Eddie tried to open the bag of cashews but it proved too stubborn. He put it back on the table.

'What happened?' he asked.

Heat flushed Larissa's cheeks. It was as though she was on an exam with all eyes on her.

'He died,' she said, looking down.

'An accident?' Eddie asked.

He appeared to be genuinely interested.

'You could say so,' Bernadette said. 'Couldn't you?'

Larissa took a long gulp of wine. 'It was a mistake,' she said. 'Could happen to anyone.'

'At least, that's what they said, right?' Bernadette said.

Larissa's elbow jerked and she almost dropped her glass.

'Anyway,' said Eddie, 'I'm glad we didn't cancel.'

'Because of David?' Bernadette asked.

'It's the third time he's flaked out.'

'Not unusual, it's the end of the semester,' Bernadette said. 'I'm surprised he's coming at all.'

They drank some wine.

'So how does this work?' Larissa asked. 'This dinner thing?'

'Oh,' Eddie said. 'Bernie didn't say?'

'I didn't go into details,' Bernadette said, 'but she knows the basics, right?'

Lara blinked at her, then turned to Eddie.

'Basically, we do this once a month.'

'More often if there's a reason,' Bernadette said.

'Right,' Eddie said.

'So, all the neighbours cook together?' Larissa asked.

Bernie laughed, swatting the air.

'Oh no. Nothing like that.'

'The idea is that we share the cooking and the hosting,' said Eddie. 'Everyone prepares something at their house.'

'Then, we move from one place to another, till we're done,' Bernadette said.

Larissa drank more wine. It didn't taste so bad once you got used to it. She was happy she'd misunderstood Bernadette and brought the cake with her. There's no way she could let people into her house, not before she'd tidied up. Clothes were still drying in the middle of her kitchen, and she'd hardly had the time to settle in. She didn't even want to think about all the other stuff.

'What did you make?' Bernie asked.

'Just some salad,' Eddie said. 'It was a last minute improvisation.'

'An incidental salad. I like the sound of that,' Bernie said.

'I guess the Johnsons are coming soon,' Eddie said, 'or did they cancel?'

'They're coming, alright,' Bernadette said. 'Fashionably late, as always.'

Larissa glanced at the clock. It was only fifteen minutes past eight, but if there was more food to be had, she wouldn't argue. Gummy olives and sour wine hardly made for an appetiser.

'Not sure we should reward them by staying,' Bernadette said. 'If you ask me—'

Hearing the doorbell, she paused.

'That must be them,' Eddie said.

'Andrew, Sylvia, you're right on time. Eddie's made a salad,' Bernadette said. 'We should eat it before it turns stale.'

∾

Appetiser

As they walked to Eddie's house, he wondered if he'd have enough time for a game or two after dinner. Another win could get him on Becca's good side again, especially if he presented it together with two tickets for her favourite spa.

He unlocked the door and almost trampled on Becca's brooch. It was the golden lily blossom he'd given her for her birthday. Eddie picked it up and put it on the sideboard in the hallway.

'You're not putting us on a diet, are you, Eddie?' asked Andrew Johnson.

'I didn't have time to go to the store,' Eddie said. 'It's a decent salad, though.'

'Andy's only teasing you,' Sylvia Johnson said. 'He loves a good salad.'

The Johnsons were starting to annoy him. He was glad he hadn't bothered to make something more elaborate. With them, there was always something to pick up on. The last time it had been Becca's hair; this time it was his salad. It was almost as if they could only be happy if they had someone to make fun of.

Eddie showed people into the living room. Sylvia shook her perky bob.

'Is Becca not coming?'

'She had to work,' Bernie said.

'Someone has to pay for the salad,' Andrew said.

Eddie wondered whether he was trying to be ironic or to point out that Becca was always working. He decided to pretend to not hear the comment.

When everyone sat down, Eddie put the salad bowl on the table. He took the wine out of the fridge.

'I know you guys prefer red, but this Sauvignon is all I've got,' he said.

There was a strange satisfaction in ruining the Johnsons' pleasure of being dissatisfied with something.

Larissa's eyes lit up when he poured the wine. Eddie added an extra splash into her glass. She didn't seem to mind.

Bernie took about a third of all the salad and licked her lips.

'Now, that's what I call an appetiser.'

'Aren't we waiting for David?' Andrew asked.

'He's solving some problems,' Bernie said.

'Not mathematical ones, I hope,' Sylvia chuckled. She served the salad to Andrew and herself.

Eddie couldn't shake off the feeling that the Johnsons were acting stranger than usual. They'd always been cheesy but did they have a reason to be cheerful? He'd stopped following Sylvia's Facebook posts because they seemed too desperate to prove what a good time she was having. At Eddie's work, people who asked for a loan or wanted to open an account rarely said more than they had to. If they did, he would start to suspect they were covering something up.

As Eddie was ready to take some salad, the doorbell rang.

'Who could that be?' Andrew said.

Eddie could see David's orange scarf through the glass in the door. David put his hand on Eddie's shoulder when he got in.

'Thanks for stepping in,' he said. He wore a shirt and a sleek black jacket and smelled of expensive cologne.

'We just started,' Eddie said.

'So, what's her name?' Sylvia asked.

'I wish.' David sat down. 'My cleaner had to take care of her father so she took some time off.'

'What's wrong with him?' Larissa asked.

'Pneumonia or something,' David said.

'Are you telling us your place is a mess?' Bernie asked.

David took some salad. Eddie noticed there was hardly any left for him.

'Trust me,' David said. 'I'd rather be cooking for you guys than sorting out my junk.'

'Well, you'd better clear out those beer cans and pizza boxes and whatever else you have there,' Bernie said. 'Next time, you're doing the main.'

'You know he'll order pizza,' Sylvia said.

David turned to Larissa.

'Are you the new Yolanda?' he asked.

'Larissa,' she said quietly.

Her wine glass was almost empty so Eddie refilled it.

'He didn't mean it like that,' Sylvia said. 'It's only because you bought Yolanda's old house.'

'Well, I'm glad,' David said. 'Even if you only did move because of the bakery.'

'I needed a change,' Larissa said. She blinked at her plate as though she were ill.

'Who wouldn't, after what you've been through,' Bernie said.

Everyone turned to Larissa who'd drunk half of her wine. Eddie wished Becca were here. She was great at defusing this kind of situation. He only knew how to divert attention.

'I hear Paul might come over for a holiday,' Eddie said.

Bernie dabbed her mouth with a napkin then threw it over the salad. Such a waste.

'Excuse me,' she said and left for the bathroom.

Sylvia glared at Eddie.

'What?' Eddie asked.

'Did you really need to mention Paul?' Sylvia said. 'They only divorced a few months ago.'

'Half a year,' Andrew said.

'I thought they parted as friends,' Eddie said.

'Friends don't bring in lawyers,' Andrew said. 'Not the big-time shark type that Paul hired.'

Larissa blushed.

'We don't usually gossip like that,' Eddie said. 'It's just that Paul used to be a part of the whole dinner thing.'

'Of course, he was,' Sylvia said. 'They were married, weren't they? Poor Bernie still hasn't gotten over him.'

'That's alright,' Larissa said. Her voice was soft and sounded as if she was going to cry. 'I lost someone too.'

As Larissa pressed her napkin against her lips, Eddie noticed her hand was scratched.

'Do you have a cat?' he asked.

Larissa froze, then promptly put her hands into her lap.

'I was putting the furniture together,' she said.

When Bernie returned from the bathroom, she was mostly interested in wine. Eddie had another bottle in the fridge but he was planning to save that one for the game. Poker and wine paired well.

He felt bad about mentioning Paul, however, so he opened the bottle. The faster they finished the dinner, the sooner he'd be playing his favourite game.

Andrew kept checking his watch. He whispered something to Sylvia, who shook her head. She then turned to the table and asked, 'Anyone here seen Dr Irving recently?'

'Why do you ask?' David asked.

'Her office says they don't know when she'll be back,' Sylvia said.

'She sometimes does this,' Eddie said. 'Goes on holiday last minute. Usually for a few weeks.'

'Isn't there someone else?' Bernie asked. 'There's this young one from the capital.'

'The hot one, you mean?' Sylvia asked. 'No, our Tammy wants Dr Irving. She'll have to wait, I guess.'

In his mind, Eddie played a game of poker with all his

favourite cards. He found that visualising the game helped him win. He had to win. Had to.

The silence around Eddie made him realise everyone was looking at him. Their plates were empty, except for Bernie's, who didn't look like she wanted to eat more.

'If you guys want to move on,' Eddie said, unsure how to finish the sentence, 'I'll just put away the plates.'

'We can help,' Sylvia said.

Eddie stood up and started to collect the empty plates. 'The dishwasher is almost full. I'll just add these and start the cycle. Won't be a minute.'

No one argued. When they left, Eddie checked who'd confirmed to join the game. Most names were new, which was good. Amateurs were the easiest to beat.

Before leaving the house, Eddie took one last look at the place. His eyes paused on the hallway sideboard. Wasn't there supposed to be something there? He was sure something had been there but he couldn't remember what, so he locked the door and headed across the street to the Johnsons'.

Main Course

It wasn't that Bernie didn't enjoy Larissa's company, but there was something strange about the woman. Had she misunderstood that she was supposed to serve the cake at her place?

Bernie had gone out of her way to invite Larissa to dinner, even though she was practically letting a complete stranger into her house. Into all their houses, as a matter of fact, while Larissa hadn't even bothered to invite them over. She'd brought the cake instead.

When it became clear that Bernie would have to sit next to Sylvia or Larissa, she promptly sat down at Sylvia's side.

'Is it me or did you change something here?' Eddie asked.

Sylvia giggled and wrapped a strand of her hair around her index finger. 'You're spot on,' she said. 'Can you tell what's different?'

'This vase is new,' Bernie said.

She hated this game. The Johnsons always flaunted their stuff, almost as if they enjoyed showing off. New curtains, designer plates, their stupid crystal glasses. Not everyone could afford to buy these things. Did they ever think about that?

'The carpet, maybe?' Eddie said.

'We bought a few small things,' Sylvia said. 'Most of the stuff is old, though, just switched around.'

'Our new friend is a designer,' Andrew said.

'The one who was here last weekend?' David asked.

Sylvia's eyes widened. 'Beg your pardon?'

'I didn't mean to spy on you, but you do kind of live across the street.'

'So, you just happened to look?' Bernie asked.

Her lips lost colour. What had this town turned into? People spying on each other? Were they spying on her? She made an effort to appear positively upset.

'What can I say,' David said. 'Maths exams aren't exactly thrilling.'

Andrew poured wine. He turned the bottle towards Bernie so she could see the big golden sticker on the bottleneck. Big stinking deal. So they were serving expensive wine. Who cares?

'Don't hog your friends,' Bernie said. 'We'd love to meet them.'

With Paul having taken all his stuff, her house seemed loud and cold. She could do with some rearranging, especially if it came for free, but the Johnsons weren't listening.

'Due to popular demand…' Sylvia pointed at the massive pot on the table. Another designer item, no doubt.

'Stuffed peppers?' David asked. 'They're my favourite.'

Bernie didn't want to share the enthusiasm. Yes, their peppers were good but that's because they hardly ever made anything else.

'Andy just needs to finish the puree, don't you, sweetie?' Sylvia said.

Andrew walked over to their kitchen island and made a little performance out of mashing the potatoes. At least he was easy on the eyes. He added some milk and butter and made those silly moves young people called dancing.

Larissa was explaining something to Sylvia, who nodded.

'Oh dear,' Sylvia said. 'That couldn't have been easy.'

Bernie knew all about regret and things that could have been prevented. She wondered if she'd feel better about the whole thing if Paul had died instead. If his leaving hadn't had to do with being unhappy but with some stupid medical error, like with Larissa's fiancé.

Bernie's stomach was like a rock. Her head was dizzy. She stood up. 'Excuse me,' she said. 'I need to use the bathroom.'

Once in the bathroom, she retouched her makeup and paused in front of the mirror. The laughter that emanated from the living room made her cringe.

These were supposed to be *her* friends, yet they were clearly having much more fun when she wasn't there. It hadn't been like that when Paul was with her.

Maybe they'd prefer to have him here instead. Well, tough luck. These dinners were the one thing Paul wasn't going to take away from her.

On her way back, Bernie lingered on the hallway. Let them have fun, she thought. She'd had those peppers before and didn't have much of an appetite to begin with.

The Johnsons' bedroom was closed but smelled of incense. Had they redecorated the whole house? Surely, they wouldn't mind if she took a peek. Maybe they didn't want to introduce her to their designer friends but she could still collect some ideas just by looking.

Bernie opened the bedroom door. The crimson wall paint

seemed fresh, but apart from that, nothing else looked new except for two metal rings that were fixed into a wall. For exercise, no doubt. Andrew must be working out to keep that kind of muscle.

Bernie was about to close the door when her gaze dropped to the floor. She gasped.

Well, well, well, thought Bernie. Those chains didn't look as if they were meant for exercise, not with a leather collar attached to them. Just what did the Johnsons do with this stuff?

Bernie's heart beat hard as she shut the door. She took a few breaths and tried to make sense of what she'd seen. Had she misunderstood? She must have. They'd never.

She couldn't go back like this, though. They'd read the shock on her face. No. She had to lay her eyes on something pure and innocent, something that would restore her faith in her friends and neighbours.

Tammy's room was right beside the main bedroom. Bernie knew for a fact that Tammy was away. She poked her head into the room and almost fell over.

Darkness. Darkness and more chains. Something like that umbrella they have on TV when they interview someone and a big tripod.

Bile pushed up from Bernie's stomach. She closed the door. They should have locked it, thought Bernie. They should have locked the whole damned house.

She tried not to look at Sylvia or Andrew when she came back. Stuffed peppers and puree were distributed equally among the plates, including hers. The sight of food made Bernie sick.

'My stomach is acting up again,' she said and sat down.

'Oh, you always say that,' David said.

'We know you can eat more than anyone else,' Andrew said.

Bernie poked the pepper with her fork. Some filling came out. The food smelled nice, but when Bernie took some in her mouth, she had to make an effort to swallow it.

'I was telling Larissa not to believe everything people say,' Sylvia said.

Bernie realised Sylvia was talking to her.

'What are they saying?' Bernie asked.

'You know, the usual,' Sylvia said. 'Stuff about the bakery.'

'Oh, please,' Andrew said. 'As if anyone's going to believe the place is actually cursed.'

'Andrew's right,' Bernie said. 'The bakery isn't cursed. The family is.'

David laughed then stopped. No one else followed. Everyone pretended to eat.

'Don't believe me, if you don't want to,' Bernie said. 'This doesn't change the fact that the Noonans are cursed. Have been for a thousand years.'

David blew a raspberry. 'That would mean the curse would go all the way back to the times of the Vikings.'

'It does,' Bernie said.

'Did they have cake?' Sylvia asked.

'The word cake originates from there,' Bernie said. 'In Norse, kaka meant cake.'

'As far as I'm aware, nothing has been proven,' Andrew said.

'Spoken like a true lawyer,' Eddie said.

Bernie considered having some potato puree then decided to squish it with her fork and hide it in the sauce instead. At least the wine was good. She drank some more.

'Was that why it was so cheap?' Larissa said. 'I mean, it came at a very good price.'

'Don't bother with rumours,' David said. 'You're the new manager and that's what counts.'

He appeared to be flirting with Larissa, but then again, David liked to flirt. If it hadn't been his hobby, it could have been his job.

'I guess we'll have to wait and see,' Bernie said.

Larissa's cheeks were flushed, either from the wine or from all the attention she was getting. Bernie's bet was on the wine.

'God, I'm glad we're doing this,' Sylvia said. 'I thought you guys were going to cancel again.'

Bernie pressed her lips together. To use the Lord's name in vain in an unholy house on top of all...

Andrew must have caught her gaze, for he raised his glass.

'Really, guys, let's do this more often,' he said.

Everyone clinked their glasses, then people went on gobbling down the stuffed peppers.

'These are great,' Larissa said. 'Wouldn't mind the recipe.'

Bernie said nothing. She'd have a chance to figure it out herself, if she came once or twice more. With the Johnsons, it was either the stuffed peppers or the oven-baked bass. They'd once tried a roast chicken but it had come out dry and weird. Bernie had eaten it anyway.

Sylvia's phone roused Bernie from her thoughts.

'It's Tammy,' Sylvia said and retreated to the back of the living room. Did she know what her daughter was up to in her room? She had to know. Perhaps she even condoned it. What did Bernie know about modern life these days? She wouldn't mind knowing a bit less, though.

A few moments later, Sylvia returned and whispered something into Andrew's ear.

'Excuse us,' Andrew said.

They left.

Noise in the hallway made Bernie think they were moving something. Their chains, perhaps. She dared not think those were meant for Tammy. That poor, sweet girl must have suffered.

'Everything alright over there?' Eddie asked.

'Ignore us,' Andrew said. 'We won't be long.'

When Sylvia came back, she had her fake smile on.

'Tammy's not feeling well so she's coming back tonight,' Sylvia said.

Andrew waved at them while talking on his phone. He stepped out onto the terrace and closed the door.

'I'm so sorry,' Bernie said. 'But I've got this nervous bladder...' She didn't say any more because no one was listening.

Bernie went into the bathroom. The window was open and

looked out onto the same side as the terrace. Even without trying, she could hear Andrew talking.

'No, just tonight,' Andrew said.

He sounded as if he'd been smoking.

'That's right. Is that okay? Yeah, sorry to drop out like this. Yeah, next weekend is great,' he said. 'Alright, I'll tell her. Sorry again.'

Andrew lit a cigarette. Bernie flushed the toilet and returned to the table. Her plate was the only one still full. She forced a few bites down her throat and put down her cutlery, dropping her napkin so it covered the leftovers on her plate.

Her back had started to complain. She should move on. Where to, though? Larissa clearly didn't plan to welcome them into her house.

'I can't wait to try that cake,' Bernie said.

The sooner they left, the sooner she could stop thinking about the horrible stuff in Tammy's room.

'Shall I fetch it?' Larissa asked.

'Or we could eat it at your place,' Bernie said.

One look in Larissa's big eyes told Bernie she could forget about it. Hospitality counted for nothing these days.

'I'm sorry,' Larissa said. 'I'm not sure my place is presentable.'

'I know about that,' David said.

'So, what do we do?' asked Bernie.

She didn't mind going somewhere else as long as they went. Another minute longer in this house…

'Why don't we stay here?' Andrew said. 'We don't mind, do we, babe?'

Sylvia shook her bob and smiled.

'Course not.'

'Fine,' Bernie said. 'I'll go and get the cake.'

'Oh, I don't mind,' Larissa said. 'Save you the trouble.'

Bernie was too taken aback to react. Did this woman really expect Bernie to give her the house keys? What if she was a burglar? She could make a copy by pressing it into soap.

'I'd better come along. Bernie's lock can be moody,' Eddie said. 'You need to know what to do.'

Bernie sighed. 'Don't break anything,' she said and handed Eddie the keys.

∾

Dessert

When Larissa and Eddie returned with the cake, Eddie had a rattled look in his eyes. Could he have somehow found out? David couldn't tell. Larissa, the new neighbour, appeared perfectly normal, cheerful even, as she placed the cake in the middle of the table.

David didn't care much for desserts but he couldn't leave either, since he'd already come late.

'I asked for something off the menu,' Larissa said.

She opened the box. Collective silence was followed by a few coughs. The Johnsons whispered something to each other. David leaned closer to see what the fuss was about.

The cake was simple enough – chocolate with candied orange stripes on top.

'Isn't this the Dark Velvet cake?' Eddie asked.

'Don't say the name,' Sylvia said.

'What's going on?' Larissa asked. Her eyes were wide like those of rabbits, a quality David found attractive in women.

Bernie leaned over the cake and almost dipped the ends of her hair into the frosting.

'Can't be it,' Bernie said. 'There's no V on top. The oranges are just thrown on.'

Larissa seemed genuinely perplexed. David could understand why. As a newcomer, she hadn't grown up listening to stories about Dark Velvet and all the horror that cake had brought to the Noonan family.

'It's supposed to be a special recipe,' Larissa said. 'That's what the staff said.'

'A normal orange cake, then,' David said.

'Did they say if it was blood orange or regular?' Andrew asked.

'I don't know,' Larissa said.

Everyone took a step away, as if they expected the cake to throw itself at them.

'It's probably alright to have a piece,' Sylvia said.

'I'll cut it.'

David sliced a few pieces and put them on plates.

'The filling is red,' Eddie said.

David had never thought Eddie to be superstitious. The way he kept his distance from the plate made him reconsider.

'Might be a berry,' David said.

'I don't understand,' Larissa said. 'Is there a problem with the cake?'

'The thing is,' Eddie said, 'if it's the cake we think it is, then it might be cursed.'

David offered a slice to everyone but no one took it.

'Are you seriously not even going to try it?' David asked.

'I'm not big on desserts,' Bernie said and left for the bathroom.

'I've been trying to cut down on sugar,' Sylvia said.

'Yeah, me too,' said Andrew.

Eddie turned away and tapped at his phone. David shrugged and took a fork.

'I'll have a slice,' Larissa said. 'The staff will want to know what I thought.'

'Eddie?' David asked and offered a plate. 'A small one?'

Eddie was deep in thought. He looked at David, startled, said, 'I'll be right back,' and left.

David glanced through the glass part of the door to check where Eddie was going. The light on the porch came on. He could see Eddie wasn't going to his house, but back to Bernie's.

David let out a huge breath. 'He must have forgotten something,' he said to Larissa.

She wanted to pour more wine but the bottle was empty. 'Might be best to call it a night, anyway,' Larissa said.

David turned to the Johnsons for help, but they'd retreated all the way to the back and appeared to be discussing something they didn't agree on. He wouldn't mind calling it a night, either, but things could get tricky with Eddie wandering outside.

'I know where Andrew keeps the wine,' David said.

He went to the pantry and scanned over the cardboard boxes in the corner. The sticker on one of them was from a local sex shop and advertised a discount pack of condoms and lubricant. They must have taken empty boxes from a grocery store. David couldn't imagine any respectable wine seller reusing boxes from a sex shop.

After a few attempts, he found a box of wine and grabbed the first bottle available.

'There's Muscat,' he said to Larissa. 'It should work with dessert.'

Bernie came back from the bathroom and picked up her bag from the chair.

'Where's Eddie?' she asked.

'He forgot something.' David poured a glass. 'More wine?'

Bernie accepted the wine. 'He's got my keys,' she said.

A few moments later, the front door opened with a thump. Eddie walked in, clutching onto a crumpled silk scarf. He walked to Bernie and raised it as if it was a prize.

'How could you?' Eddie asked.

Bernie blinked and pulled the scarf from his hands. 'What are you doing with my scarf?'

'*Your* scarf?'

Eddie snatched the scarf back from Bernie, turned it around and pointed at the corner. 'Becca *always* cuts the tags off her clothes,' he said.

Bernie drank some wine. 'What's your point?'

Eddie's jaw tightened. 'I've never seen you wear it, either,' he said.

'Big deal, so we have the same scarf. So does half of the town. It was on sale last year.'

Eddie straightened the scarf and held it up so she could see the numbers. 'I suppose you also had our wedding date sewn on?'

David and Larissa exchanged a glance. David shrugged. Larissa drank more wine.

Bernie's knuckles turned pale. She put down her glass.

'I want to see what's in your pockets,' Eddie said.

It occurred to David that wine might be thrown in someone's face. He had some experience with that and it wasn't very pleasant. He took a few steps back. Larissa followed suit.

'Be reasonable,' Bernie said. 'We're not alone.'

'I know you took the brooch,' Eddie said. 'I put it on the sideboard and it wasn't there when I left.'

'Edward, please.'

Bernie sounded as though she was about to burst into tears. Eddie stretched out his hand.

'Bernadette,' he said coldly.

David had never seen him like this before. If he could corner an old lady like Bernadette in front of an audience, who knew what else he was capable of. David's mouth was dry. The wine didn't help.

'Let's not do this *now*,' Bernie said.

'I'll stop when you give back Becca's brooch.'

Bernie stuffed her hands into her trouser pockets and took a step back. Meanwhile, Andrew and Sylvia had stopped arguing and returned to the room. They looked at David as if he could explain what was going on. David shrugged. Larissa poured more wine.

'Eddie?' Sylvia asked. 'What's going on?'

'I'd like to know, too,' Eddie said, 'but Bernadette won't play along.'

'What's with the scarf?' Sylvia asked.

'She stole it,' Eddie said. 'God knows what else she took.'

For a second, Bernie's face distorted into what appeared to be a half-smile, but David knew better. He'd seen too many women crying to miss the signs. Moments later, she broke into a sob.

'You don't understand,' she cried out. 'Paul took everything. Even the towels and bedsheets!'

Sylvia hugged Bernie while Andrew poured more wine. He drained his glass then refilled it once more.

'Let's take a deep breath,' Andrew said. 'It's been a long day and we've all had a few drinks.'

'Why don't you make some coffee?' Sylvia said, while stroking Bernie's hair.

She managed to direct Bernie towards the sofa and made her sit down. Bernie buried her face in the crook of Sylvia's neck.

David checked the time and wondered whether this would be a good time to slip out. Everyone was here so there'd be no danger.

'Hon, didn't you buy coffee?' Andrew asked as he opened and closed all the cupboards in the kitchen.

'Didn't *you*?' Sylvia asked.

Bernie started to wail.

'I thought we still had a pack,' Andrew said.

'I might have some at home,' David said.

If he offered coffee, he could excuse himself and leave, but before he could say this, Eddie said, 'I wouldn't mind an espresso. You still have the machine, right, David?'

'Yes, but—' David said.

'Alright,' Eddie said. 'Let's go.'

'My place is quite a mess,' David said.

'I don't mind,' Eddie said.

'You could still make the coffee and bring it over,' Andrew said.

'I'd have to check if I still have some,' David said.

'I'll come with you,' Andrew said, 'in case you need help.'

'Bring me one, too,' Sylvia said.

Andrew turned to Larissa, who appeared as if she'd forgotten where she was.

'I suppose I'll come, too,' she said.

'Alright,' Andrew said. 'We'll be right back.'

'Guys, there's no need for everyone to come along,' David said.

Bernie started to howl like a wolf with pneumonia.

Andrew nodded to David, as if it was a done deal. Perhaps for Andrew, it was.

'I wonder if Eddie could…' said David.

He looked for Eddie but he'd already left. His heart sank.

'What about the cake?' Larissa asked.

'Don't worry, no one will touch it.' Andrew led her out.

David struggled to move away from the doorstep. As he watched Eddie, Andrew and Larissa head over to his house, his mind screamed.

Coffee

Andrew wasn't surprised to find David's house unlocked. The neighbourhood was safe and there was always someone on the watch. He did wonder, though, why David had left the heating ramped up to maximum. A few lights were on, too. Clearly, David didn't care about the environment or his energy bill.

The whole drama around the scarf seemed a bit much but getting involved would have only made things worse. Even if Bernie had stolen the ugly scarf, what could Andrew do? If Eddie wanted to sue, Andrew could use his work to argue why it was a poor case. In his experience, most cases were settled before they reached court. The sooner everyone calmed down and stopped being ridiculous, the sooner they could go back home.

David sprinted past Andrew and almost tripped over Larissa.

'No need to rush,' Andrew said. 'We won't clean up.'

The joke was meant to lighten the mood, but David appeared more strained now than back at their place.

Eddie whistled as he turned around.

'You call *this* a mess?' Eddie said. 'Should have seen our house when Becca's finishing her reports.'

Except for a coffee cup on the table and some half-eaten chocolate, the living room was tidy. Not quite the tower of empty pizza boxes Andrew had expected to find. Maybe David had finally started to look after himself or, maybe, someone else had.

David hurried towards his bedroom. Once there, he stopped and turned around.

'You're right,' David said. 'It's not as bad as I remember.'

Eddie turned on the coffee machine and took some espresso cups out of the cupboard. Larissa and Andrew sat down while David dawdled, as if he wasn't sure what to do next. Finally, he sat down on the sofa.

'Listen, Eddie,' Andrew said. 'I don't know what happened with Bernie, but—'

Eddie turned.

'She's a thief, that's what happened,' he said.

'Even if she took that scarf,' Andrew said, 'is it really worth more than friendship?'

Eddie didn't respond. Instead, he lined up the cups and counted them, added one more, then started to make coffee.

At the sound of a car, Andrew turned to the window. It was too soon for Tammy to be back, though. At least he and Sylvia had managed to move their toys back into their own bedroom. Having their daughter walk in on their sex party would have been awkward, to say the least.

'If you expect me to just forget about this...' Eddie said.

'Not forget,' Andrew said, 'but you should be able to talk, once things calm down.'

'She nicked the brooch, too, the one I got Becca for her birthday. Can you believe that? Who knows what else she stole?'

Andrew helped Eddie bring the coffee to the table. They were bringing the last cups, when Eddie paused midway. He put down the coffee and squinted at the door. 'Is that... Becca's coat?'

David leaped up but Eddie had already made his way to the coat rack. He pulled the coat off the hook and lifted it for everyone to see. It was a camel-coloured coat that looked like Becca's.

'What's it doing here?' Eddie asked.

'One of the teachers must have forgotten it,' David said.

'Teachers?' Eddie asked.

'I host our monthly natural science meeting,' David said.

He reached for the coat but Eddie wouldn't give it away. He inspected the lining.

'Are you sure?' Eddie asked. 'Becca always clips off the tag. Like this, see?'

David clenched his jaw. That's when Andrew knew.

'We've all got a bit excited,' Andrew said. 'Let's have the coffee and—'

Eddie threw the coat at David.

'She's here, isn't she?' Eddie asked.

'Eddie, please,' David said.

'Let's not jump to any conclusions,' Andrew said.

No one was listening.

Eddie marched down the corridor and shouted 'Becca?' at each closed door.

'She's not here, man,' David said.

Andrew could swear a lock had turned somewhere. He said nothing, though. Eddie opened each door as David and Andrew followed him. Larissa stayed at the back.

The last door was the bedroom. It door didn't open. Eddie rapped his fingers on the wood.

'Becca?'

'Eddie,' David said.

'Why is it locked, huh?' Eddie asked.

'It's where I keep the tests. Some students come here for extra classes. I don't want to take any risks.'

'No danger now, is there?' Eddie said. 'Go ahead. Unlock it.'

'Eddie,' David said in the tone of a disappointed parent.

'The only reason to keep it locked is because you're hiding something.'

Eddie banged on the door. 'Becca?'

Andrew put his hand on Eddie's shoulder. Eddie promptly shook it off. He seemed determined to plunge from one drama to the next. Things weren't supposed to escalate, not when Andrew had come along to diffuse the whole situation. Sylvia would be livid if he didn't manage to calm things down. Then again, he wouldn't have minded some angry sex after all this. It was when Sylvia was at her best.

'Come on, Eddie. Let's drink the coffee and go back,' Andrew said.

'Someone open this fucking door!'

Andrew arched his eyebrows at David, who shrugged. He could see in David's eyes that Eddie was right. If Eddie found out that Becca was behind the door, who knew what he'd do.

'Fine,' David said, 'if you want to be dramatic.'

Eddie folded his arms and glared while David fumbled with the key. He inserted it into the lock but it got stuck halfway.

'Seems it's jammed,' David said. 'I'll need to get that fixed.'

He took out his phone.

'It's jammed because someone jammed it from the inside,' Eddie said. He peeked through the keyhole. 'Something moved!'

Eddie snatched the key from David's hands and kicked at the door.

'If you don't open this bloody door, I'll kick it down, I swear.'

'Woah, woah, woah,' Andrew pulled Eddie away. 'Let's take a deep one here, shall we? No need to get violent.'

'You know I can do it,' Eddie shouted at the door.

Something tripped and fell on the other side of the door.

'Becca! Open up this very second, or I swear I will—'

The lock turned and the door opened with a screech. Becca was wearing David's dressing gown and, it seemed, not much else underneath.

'Or you will what?' Becca asked calmly.

Larissa hiccupped. Everyone turned.

'It's getting late,' Larissa said.

Andrew rushed to her. 'Would you mind sticking around for just a bit?' he whispered. 'To make sure nothing goes wrong?'

Larissa sighed, but she seemed to have given in. Becca and Eddie glared at each other.

'How long has this been going on?' Eddie asked.

'How long has our marriage been falling apart?' Becca asked.

Eddie's face dropped. His shoulders slumped.

'Is this what you want?' Eddie asked.

Andrew held his breath. The whole room seemed to be waiting to exhale.

'You'd know what I want, if you ever listened to me,' Becca said.

'I do listen to you,' he said.

David tried to leave but Larissa was blocking the way.

Perhaps things weren't as bad as they seemed. After all, when this was over, Becca and Eddie, or maybe even Becca and David, would open their minds to other things, too.

'If you did, you wouldn't have gambled away our savings,' Becca said, 'and thought you could make things better with your stupid presents.'

Eddie looked down and pushed his hands into his pockets. He pulled out the ugly silk scarf he'd taken from Bernie.

'You didn't think this was stupid when I gave it to you,' he said.

'Eddie. Don't.'

'I guess the brooch was stupid too, huh?'

'This isn't the place, Eddie.'

'If it's stupid, then you wouldn't care if I gave it all away, would you?'

Becca propped her hand on her hip. 'We'll talk when I get home.'

'What's the bloody point?' Eddie said. 'Seems you've already decided it's over.'

'I think what Becca is trying to say…' Andrew said.

Becca shook her head. 'No, Eddie's right,' she said. 'He can't fix this any longer. No one can.'

The scarf dropped from Eddie's hands.

'Fine,' he said. 'Since you've decided to leave, I'll pack your stuff.'

'Eddie,' Andrew said. 'There's no need to do anything right now. If we all just took a moment and—'

Eddie turned his narrow, fuming eyes on Andrew. 'Fuck this,' he said. 'If that's how she wants to have it, fine with me. I'll be just fine with what I make at poker.'

He turned to Becca. 'I'll get rid of all those stupid presents you said you didn't want.'

'Be my guest,' Becca said.

For a moment, no one moved. The air was charged. Andrew's gut was pulsing. Then Becca said, 'Well, what are you waiting for?'

Eddie turned and left, slamming the door behind him. It felt to Andrew as if someone had stopped pushing him to the ground.

'I need a drink,' he said.

'What if he comes back?' Larissa asked. 'What if he turns violent?'

'He won't,' Andrew said. 'But you're right. We shouldn't stay here, just in case.'

They all glanced at each other. Andrew felt he needed to spell things out.

'Well, Bernie is still at our place,' he said.

'He's not a maniac,' Becca said, 'but we can't go to our house either.'

Andrew looked at Larissa. 'I guess that leaves your place.'

'I've got nothing to offer,' Larissa said.

David opened a cupboard and took out a bottle of brandy. He handed it to Larissa.

'Here,' he said. 'Take this.'

'I could use a stiff one,' Becca said. 'I'll get dressed.'

Larissa smiled sourly. It seemed to Andrew that the blush had disappeared from her cheeks.

∾

Brandy

Becca put on David's shirt and fastened a belt around her waist so it looked like a dress. She put on shoes and took her coat.

'Shall we?'

It was a short walk. Becca appreciated the fresh air. Spending the evening locked in David's bedroom wasn't exactly her idea of a good time.

Andrew and David rushed ahead, while she and the new neighbour lagged behind.

'I'm sorry,' Becca said. 'I didn't catch your name.'

'Larissa,' the woman said.

She didn't seem to be in a hurry to be anywhere.

Andrew and David were discussing something, but Becca couldn't hear what although the way David wrung his hands and stared at his feet made Becca sure it was to do with Eddie. At least she and David no longer had to hide. The past year had been as nerve racking as it was exciting.

'You should talk to them,' Larissa said. 'I don't think it's a good idea to go anywhere right now.'

Becca found this a strange comment, since Andrew and David were already at Yolanda's old house.

'We won't stay long,' Becca said. 'I can help,' she added, though she wasn't quite sure what she could help with.

'That's alright,' Larissa said.

She took out her keys and stared at them for a few moments. Becca's fingers turned numb from the cold. It was colder outside than she cared to admit.

Andrew rubbed his arms. 'Don't let us freeze.'

Larissa sighed, inserted the key and turned it very slowly.

Inside, the house didn't seem much warmer than outside. Becca buttoned up her coat. The harsh white light made the place look like a warehouse. So did the cardboard boxes that were scattered all over the floor. Becca recognised the sticker from a big furniture shop. Some boxes were duct taped and labelled with a marker. Since there weren't any chairs, Becca sat down on one of the boxes.

'I didn't have a chance to settle in,' Larissa said.

She got a few dusty glasses out of a box and took them to the sink. Andrew helped wash and distribute the glasses.

'If you need help putting this stuff together…' David said.

Becca glared at him. They hadn't even had a chance to talk about what they wanted to do, now that they could, and here he was, offering his free time to assemble someone else's furniture.

'There are also services that can help with that,' Becca said.

They'd need to straighten a few things out if this relationship was going to work.

'That's alright,' Larissa said. 'I don't mind doing it myself, I just need some time.'

Andrew poured a good measure of brandy into each glass.

'If you don't mind me asking,' he said, 'will you two be moving in together?'

'Well,' David said.

'Probably, for the time being,' Becca said.

She wasn't too crazy about the idea but paying for a hotel seemed outrageous too. Once she and Eddie sold the house, she'd buy a flat. Rent it out, if things went well.

The brandy stung Becca's throat, but it left a nice, fuzzy taste in her mouth.

'I suppose Eddie will come around, eventually,' Andrew said.

'I wouldn't be surprised if he didn't,' Becca said. 'I've been trying to tell him for a while, now. Haven't I, David?'

David drew in a long breath.

'He never tried to quit, then?' Andrew asked.

'I don't want to talk about Eddie,' Becca said.

She turned to Larissa for support, but Larissa was staring at her glass, as if her mind was somewhere else.

'Well, if you need a place to stay,' Andrew said.

'My stuff is at David's anyway,' Becca said.

'Yeah.' David shifted in his chair.

The doorbell sounded like a parrot choking. Larissa got up, her drink still in her hands.

'If it's Eddie...' David said.

'I doubt it,' Becca said.

Larissa unlocked the door.

'So, that's where the party is,' Sylvia said. She pointed at Larissa's glass. 'Any more where this came from?'

Andrew poured a glass and gave it to her. Sylvia sat down.

'What got into Eddie?' she asked. 'He stormed in with bags of stuff and gave it all to Bernie.'

'What did she do?'

'They shouted at each other for a while, then Bernie left and Eddie went back home.'

Sylvia took a sip of brandy then turned to Becca. 'You're here!'

Her gaze slipped from Becca's coat to her almost bare legs. Then she glanced at David, who kept his head down.

'In any case,' Sylvia said. 'Cheers.'

They drank the brandy. Larissa took the bottle and held it up.

'Does anyone want more of this?' she asked.

There were a few shrugs, so she made another round and emptied the rest of the bottle into her glass.

Becca wondered why she was in such a rush. It was then that she heard a muffled sound.

'What was that?' Becca asked.

'What was what?' Andrew asked.

They paused. If Becca concentrated, she could hear a subdued sound, as if someone was knocking next door.

'That,' Becca said.

She stood up.

'I don't hear anything,' Larissa said.

'Becca's right,' Sylvia said and put down her glass. 'I can hear it, too. Sounds like a rat.'

Something tripped and rolled on the floor. A faint squeak resembled a bird's cry.

'Must be the crickets,' Larissa said.

'Not in winter,' Becca said.

'Sounds almost like a person,' Sylvia said.

The squeak came back. If Becca hadn't known any better, she'd have said it sounded like someone saying 'elf'.

'You sure we're alone?' David asked. 'I mean, if Eddie tried to—'

'Give it a break, will you?' Becca said. 'What are you so afraid of? Eddie couldn't even kill a mosquito.'

There was a loud thump, as though something had bumped against the door. Andrew put down his drink.

'We'd better go and check.'

Andrew headed down the corridor. Becca reached out to David. Reluctantly, he took her hand and followed.

As they walked on, the thumps became more frequent and pronounced.

'Maybe it's a bat,' Sylvia said and reached for Andrew's hand. 'It happened to us last year.'

The more Becca listened, the more it seemed to her as if someone was saying 'Help'.

Somewhere in the back, a lock turned. Andrew kicked open each door but found nothing except more boxes and empty rooms.

'Is someone smoking?' Sylvia asked.

Andrew kicked the last door open. Something rolled out into the corridor.

Becca covered her mouth.

'Dear Lord,' said Sylvia. 'Is that Dr Irving?'

On the floor was a woman, gagged and tied up with rope and duct tape. Andrew untied her.

'What are you doing here?' he asked.

The moment he ripped the duct tape off Dr Irving's mouth, the doctor cried out. 'Call the police!'

'What the hell is going on?' David asked.

'She's crazy. Thinks I killed her fiancé. You need to help me,' Dr Irving said.

'Larissa?' Andrew asked.

No one answered.

'Where did she go?' Sylvia asked.

'She was here a second ago,' Andrew said.

'Quick, David,' Becca said, 'give me your phone.'

Her chest was thundering. She struggled to get enough air.

'I left it at home,' David said.

'Fine, any phone,' Becca said. 'Anyone?'

'I didn't take mine,' Andrew said.

Sylvia helped untie Dr Irving.

'It's okay,' Andrew said. 'Let's just go back.'

He tried to open the front door. It was locked.

'What do we do?' David asked.

Becca was turning to respond when her jaw dropped. Heaps of smoke rolled towards her. Light danced oddly around the door, as though multiple torches were trying to get through. It was then that she noticed the flames, leisurely licking the sides of the doorframe.

THE RECIPES

The recipes in this collection are an eclectic bunch and follow the order of the short stories. Most dishes are simple and easy to make. Those who hoped for an elaborate recipe from the 'Moments' menu might be disappointed. As I have never had a chance to eat there, I had to dream up all the dishes. However, if there's a dish from the stories you're dying to make, let me know.

The dishes presented here include my absolute favourites, like 'The Forbidden Pasta', 'Stuffed Peppers' and 'The Courgette Strudel'. The latter elbowed its way into two separate stories. While I am not a chef, I am a pretty decent cook and a person who loves food. I enjoy trying out new flavours and dishes and take pleasure in my food. Though I can imagine that after publishing a book called *Add Cyanide to Taste,* demand for my cooking skills might plummet.

Almost all recipes are related to the short stories. Almost? There's a loose one, strolling around, looking for a home. Maybe you'll find a good story for it. If you do, drop me a line. I'd love to read it. If you're one of those readers who enjoys their stories with some food, I'd absolutely love to see what you're eating while reading this book. I'll be sharing my photos under the hashtag #Cyanide2Taste. I look forward to seeing yours.

Before you cook away, let me share a piece of Mum's wisdom. Take the time and create a good mood. I often cook with music. It's always best to listen to music you like. If you feel adventurous, though, look up my 'Add Cyanide to Taste' playlist on Spotify. It includes a list of songs that birthed, inspired or reflected this short story collection.

Needless to say, please don't add cyanide to any of the dishes.

JANICE'S PUMPKIN GNOCCHI

Most people have had at least one job where they had to work for a horrible boss like Bert Oxley. I hope some were able to face it with Janice's grace and tenacity, minus the murder, of course. When I tried to question Janice about her preferred foods, she was very evasive. So, I did what any self-respecting writer would do and followed her around until she got hungry and sat down to eat. The one thing I can tell you about Janice is that I've never seen her eat a piece of meat.

She does like a bit of variety in food, that's why this pumpkin gnocchi recipe comes with three different sauce options. The gnocchi themselves are my variation on existing recipes, many of which I liked, yet thought could be further improved. Roasting the pumpkin instead of boiling it, for example, reduces the moisture and intensifies the taste.

This recipe is for two good eaters or three normal eaters. The gnocchi also freeze very well and make for a delicious surprise when your fridge is empty and you're about to use the corkscrew to open a can of expired vegetables you found in the pantry.

Time needed: about 2 hours to make the gnocchi and another 15 minutes for the sauce

Pumpkin gnocchi ingredients for 6:
300g roasted pumpkin
150g roasted sweet potato (about 1)
620g plain flour, plus some for dusting
100g full-fat ricotta
30g grated parmesan cheese
1 egg
½ tsp salt
a good grind of pepper
olive oil

Warm the oven to 220 °C.

Scoop the seeds out of the pumpkin and cut it into slices as wide as your palm. There's no need to peel it, as you'll be scooping out the flesh once it's baked. Cut the sweet potato in half, add to the tray and drizzle the vegetables with olive oil. Roast for about 45-50 minutes, until they begin to brown.

Once the vegetables are done, scoop out the flesh and put it into a big bowl. Allow it to cool down before you mash it into a pulp with a hand mixer. Add salt, pepper, ricotta, parmesan and egg and mix. Gradually add flour until the dough comes together. The final amount of flour will depend on how moist your pumpkin mash is. Use a stand mixer with a dough hook on a low speed or do it by hand. If the pumpkin is on the moist side, you might need to add more flour. Eventually you'll get a dough that is soft but mouldable. When done, the dough might still be a bit sticky but if you dust it in more flour, it will be of a similar consistency to bread dough. If you don't make bread, then squeeze your earlobe – the dough should feel roughly the same.

Take a handful of dough and put it on a dusted surface. With your fingers, mould the dough into a roll, starting at the middle and expanding towards the edges. Once you get a roll about the size of a hotdog, slice it into gnocchi-sized pieces. Press the back of a fork against each piece to create creases for the sauce to stick onto.

Boil the gnocchi in water – they are done after a few minutes or when they rise to the surface. Drain the gnocchi before adding them to a sauce of your choice. All three sauces are established recipes that I love making but can't take any credit for.

If you end up with some leftover pumpkin puree, spice it with some salt, pepper and a pinch of nutmeg, and eat as a side dish.

Sage Butter Sauce for 2

Time needed: 10 minutes

Ingredients:
25 sage leaves
50g butter
salt, pepper to taste

Melt the butter over a low flame and add cooked and drained gnocchi and sage leaves. Fry them until they start to brown, add salt and pepper to taste and serve while still hot.

Sorrentina Sauce for 2

Time needed: 15 minutes

Ingredients:
1 tbsp canola oil
1 brown onion (100 g), chopped
60g mozzarella, cut into pieces

300ml tomato puree
1 tbsp fresh oregano (or 1 tsp dried)
a few leaves of fresh basil
salt, pepper to taste

Fry the onion in oil and add salt and oregano. When the onion becomes transparent, add tomato puree and mozzarella. Allow the cheese to start melting, then turn off the heat. Add fresh pepper, pour the sauce over the gnocchi and decorate with fresh basil leaves.

Feta and Tomato Sauce for 2

Time needed: 15 minutes

Ingredients:
1 tbsp canola oil
2 cloves of garlic, finely sliced
150g feta, cubed
300g cherry tomatoes, halved
salt, pepper to taste

Fry the garlic in oil. Add cherry tomatoes. Allow the tomatoes to start falling apart, then add feta. After the cheese melts, take off heat and serve with the gnocchi.

BERT OXLEY'S ROAST CHICKEN

This is the only dish in the collection I haven't tasted, because I don't eat meat. My husband enthusiastically offered to help out. I'm beginning to suspect it was not only for the purposes of this book. We didn't necessarily agree on Bert Oxley's eating habits, e.g. whether he'd order a whole chicken (I think he would) and what he'd do with the leftovers. My guess was he'd take the doggy bag for his pet. My husband thought he wasn't the type to have a pet. I'm afraid he's right. Even Bert Oxley can't finish a whole chicken and he probably wouldn't give a damn about food waste.

Nevertheless, I hope Oxley's fate won't deter you from preparing this dish.

Time needed: about 1.5 - 2 hours

Ingredients:
1 chicken
½ lemon (organic and washed well)
1 sprig of oregano
1 sprig of thyme

1 tsp pepper
1 tsp salt
1 tsp sweet paprika powder
½ tsp allspice
½ tsp dry oregano
olive oil

Preheat the oven to 200 °C and choose an oven dish big enough to fit the chicken. You'll also want to weigh the chicken to estimate its cooking time.

Coat the oven dish with a thin layer of olive oil. Mix the spices and add half of them to the oil layer. Add the twig of oregano and thyme to the bottom of the oven dish. Place the chicken in the dish with the breast up. Put the lemon inside the chicken. Liberally massage the chicken with the olive oil until it's covered. This will make the difference between ending up with a dry chicken or a juicy one. Sprinkle the rest of the spices over the chicken.

For the roasting, I recommend following Nigella Lawson's formula: 20 minutes per ½ kilo of chicken plus an additional 30 minutes. So, for 1 kg of chicken, this would mean you'd have to roast it in the oven for 70 minutes. Once the time is up, switch off the oven and let the chicken rest in there for another 20 minutes.

HOT CHOCOLATE

Many things pass as hot chocolate these days, whether they include actual chocolate or not. After living in Belgium, I've learned to appreciate the flavour of actual chocolate, so here's my own perfect cup of hot chocolate, inspired by Cristina Tosi's milky creations. To make a vegan version, substitute milk for an oat/soy beverage.

Time needed: 10 minutes

Ingredients for 1 cup:
40g dark chocolate (70% cocoa content or higher)
250ml milk, in which you've soaked your favourite granola/cereal
½–1 tsp vanilla sugar
a pinch of cinnamon
a pinch of ground cardamom
a tiny pinch of salt

Soak your favourite cereal or granola in milk for 10–15 minutes. Eat the granola and put the milk into a small pot together with the chocolate. Heat over a low to medium flame.

Once the chocolate starts to melt, take the pot off the heat and put the milk with chocolate into a blender. A hand mixer works too. Mix the chocolate and milk till there's no more chocolate visible, usually around a minute.

Add the sugar and spices. If you like your chocolate sweet, you can skip the salt and add more sugar. Enjoy your hot chocolate.

BLUEBERRY SCHNAPPS

In Slovenia, almost anything that grows can be put into schnapps and called a home remedy. I did not initially intend to include this recipe in the book but I reconsidered after a friend read 'Three Roses' and said he'd like to try it.

Since my mum makes excellent blueberry schnapps, I asked her for a recipe. As it's often the case, Mum's recipes aren't exact science, so you might have to adjust the quantities as you see fit, depending on how much schnapps you want to make.

I advise not skimping on the blueberries. The more there are, the tastier the schnapps. The best thing about this drink is that after you've had it, you can eat the blueberries.

Time needed: 2–3 weeks

Ingredients for one bottle:
500g fresh blueberries
sugar
a bottle of quality plum schnapps or vodka
a mason jar
an empty bottle

Put blueberries into a jar, about 3 cm thick from the bottom, then put a good spoon of sugar over them. Add another blueberry layer followed by sugar and repeat this until the mason jar is full. Close the jar and leave it in a sunny spot, e.g. a windowsill.

Monitor the jar's contents, opening it every few days and shaking it gently before closing the jar. When the blueberries start to ooze, they're ready to be introduced to the schnapps, usually after two to three weeks. It's important to stop the process before the blueberries ferment, so keep an eye on them.

Once your blueberry sugar mix is nice and oozy, transfer them into a bottle and add the schnapps/vodka. Leave to rest for a few days before serving.

SARAH'S POSH CHEESE SANDWICH

Those who expected to get the recipe for Ula's amazing curry might be disappointed at finding only Sarah's cheese sandwich. Truth be told, I never trusted Ula's curry, so the cheese sandwich seemed like the right way to go.

The spicy mayonnaise is based on Meera Sodha's kimchi mayonnaise recipe and is only slightly improved with a spoon of mustard. If you'd still rather eat something curry-like, I strongly recommend looking up Meera Sodha's *East* which became one of my favourite cookbooks.

Time needed: 15 minutes

Ingredients for 1 sandwich:
half a baguette
a few slices of fresh parmesan cheese (best borrowed from your chef flatmate)
½ ripe avocado
2–3 tbsp spicy mayo

Ingredients for the spicy mayo:
50g kimchi

100g mayonnaise
1 tsp mustard

Cut the baguette in half lengthwise. Scoop the avocado out and spread it over the lower part. Blend the spicy mayo ingredients together in a food processor. Add a few spoons of spicy mayo and slices of fresh parmesan to the sandwich.

My husband likes to 'improve' the sandwich by adding a few slices of gabagool (aka capocollo/coppa), but I assure you the sandwich is quite delicious without it too. Enjoy.

FIONA'S CHOCOLATE MISO COOKIES

This is my first ever cookie recipe, and though Fiona wouldn't have gone to this much trouble to feed Betty, I can imagine she'd have a stash of them ready for moments when you just need something sweet. As I'm not much of a sweet tooth, these cookies combine sweet with savoury. If you make them, leave one out for a potential house ghost. I hear they appreciate such offerings.

Time needed: about 20 minutes to prepare and 15–20 minutes to bake

Ingredients for 16–18 cookies:
200g unsalted butter, cubed
100g sugar
2 eggs
250g flour
50g almond powder
1 tbsp miso paste
1 tsp baking soda
1 tsp cornstarch
200g dark chocolate chips
150g chopped nuts of your choice

Preheat the oven to 210 °C.

Mix sugar and cubed butter with a stand mixer or a hand mixer on middle speed, till they turn creamy. Add the eggs and miso paste. When you have more or less a smooth mass, add almonds, flour, baking soda and cornstarch. Continue mixing at a low speed.

The dough you get will be sticky but mouldable. Turn off the mixer and add the nuts. I like to use cashews, but walnuts, almonds, pistachios or any other nuts are alright. Well, perhaps not a coconut. Add chocolate chips. I tend to take two bars of dark chocolate of 75–80 % cocoa and chop it with a knife.

Mix well, so the chocolate and nuts distribute and integrate into the dough.

You can make the cookies either with your hand, or by using an ice-cream scoop – scoop the dough into your hand and flatten it. A single ball of dough will weigh roughly between 70 and 80g, which makes for quite a large cookie.

Leave quite some space between the cookies when you put them on a baking tray, as they will expand during baking.

Bake for 15–20 minutes and let cool down before you collect them as they will be soft. However, nothing is stopping you from scooping one of them out and munching on it while still warm.

APRICOT PIE

This pie is a variation on the French 'Fondant aux pommes', a recipe made especially for this short story collection, as it appears in 'The Recipe'.

Since I was working on this dish while living in Brazil, acquiring apricots was somewhat challenging. For this reason, I know that this recipe also works if you substitute apricots with plums, apples or peaches. Thanks to my mum, I can confirm that it also works with apricots as she was kind enough to double-test this recipe for me. If you're not a fan of apricots, feel free to substitute them for apples (thinly sliced), strawberries, blueberries or any other fruit.

The best thing about this pie? It doesn't contain cyanide :)

Time needed: about 15 minutes to prepare and 25 minutes to bake

Ingredients for 6–8:
10 apricots, pitted and halved (fresh or from a preserve)
50g butter
1 egg
250g Greek yoghurt (full fat)

100g plain flour
100g sugar
40g almond flour
2 tsp baking powder
a pack of vanilla sugar (or real vanilla for extra decadence)
a pinch of salt
a splash of rum (optional)

Preheat the oven to 180 °C.

Melt butter and let it cool. In a big bowl, whisk egg, sugar and vanilla sugar, till they become creamy. Mix in yoghurt with a big spoon. Slowly add flour and almond flour till you get a smooth texture. Add vanilla, salt and baking powder and mix some more. Finally, add cooled melted butter and, if you wish, a splash of rum.

Spread the batter over a pie mould, about 28cm in diameter.

With the cut half down, arrange the apricots over the mould and bake for 25–30 minutes. Allow the pie to cool down before serving it.

COURGETTE STRUDEL

This dish is among my absolute favourites – another creation of my genius mum. You might frown at the idea of a savoury strudel but I assure you that this baby is perfect for a snack or a full meal, if served with salad. I love to have a few slices when it's still warm from the oven. It'll keep for a short while in the fridge without losing any of its moisture and yumminess. You can tell I wanted this recipe to be included in the book as it's the only one that appears in two stories.

Time needed: about 2 hours

Ingredients for the dough:
600g fine white flour
200ml lukewarm water
1 tbsp apple vinegar
½ tsp salt
1 egg
2–3 tbsp oil

Mix the salt, vinegar and water together and add to the flour. You can knead the dough with your hands or with a mixer. Gradually add the egg and the oil. The dough should be relatively soft and elastic but will be a bit harder and less puffy than bread dough.

Shape four loaves, cover them with a cloth and let them rest for about 30 minutes. Once the dough is ready, roll it out roughly to a size a bit bigger than an A5 sheet, brush with oil and let rest for 5 minutes. If you're running low on space, you can fold the dough while it rests. After 5 minutes, stretch the dough with your hands so you end up with rather thin dough.

Ingredients for the filling:
1–1.5 kg courgette, peeled and grated
½ tbsp salt
500g cottage cheese
150g sour cream or Greek yoghurt
2 eggs
2tsp salt
1–2 tbsp polenta (if needed)
butter shavings (optional)
oil for brushing
butter
breadcrumbs

Preheat the oven to 200 °C.

Mix the grated courgette with the salt and let rest for 5 to 10 minutes, so the courgette releases water. Use a sieve or a clean cloth to squeeze the water out of the courgettes. Add the cottage cheese, sour cream, eggs and salt. Mix and taste the filling. Add salt to taste. The filling should be roughly the same consistency as potato puree. If it's too runny and looks like it might be difficult to roll intro strudel, add 1 to 2tbsp polenta. You can add a few shavings of butter into the filling.

Spread the filling over the dough, then carefully roll each dough – starting with the side closest to you – outwards. If you have difficulties, try placing the dough on baking paper and lift it slightly to help the rolling. Scoop any leftover filling into a dish and bake it with the strudel, as it makes for a nice snack.

Grease the oven dish with butter and sprinkle with breadcrumbs. Place the strudel rolls on the dish and brush with oil.

Bake the strudel for around 50 minutes until it browns.

OVEN-BAKED PANCAKES

My mum's oven-baked pancakes are the kind of dish that make you lick your fingers. The only problem – insofar as you could call it that – that she cooks for about ten people. Though there are plenty of volunteers to help fight the food waste, I tried to scale it down.

As with most of my mum's recipes, this one, too, needed some guesswork around the quantities. To a seasoned cook, instructions along the lines of 'add enough flour to make the right consistency' might make sense. To others, not really.

So, here's my slightly tweaked version, mostly because I prefer my pancakes semi-sweet and because I couldn't easily get sour cream in Brazil. The ingredients are for two people and should yield about four pancakes. I find it impossible to eat only one. Technically, you could serve one pancake per person, but why would you want to do that? Once their scent seduces you and you take the first bite, you might be tempted to…

Can you hear a new story ticking in the back of my mind?

Time needed: about 1 hour

Ingredients for the pancakes:
1 egg
200ml milk
90g flour
1 tbsp sugar
1tsp vanilla sugar
pinch of salt
oil

Preheat the oven to 200 °C.

Whisk together all the pancake ingredients, except for the oil, and make 4 pancakes in a non-stick frying pan. Set aside.

Ingredients for the filling:
250g cottage cheese
70g ricotta (or sour cream)
1 egg
2 tbsp raisins
1 tsp vanilla sugar
½ tsp cinnamon
pinch of salt
butter (for greasing the oven dish)

Mix all the ingredients for the filling together. Feel free to add more sugar into the filling if you like life on the sweet side. Add two to three tablespoons of filling onto each pancake. Roll the pancakes and place into a greased oven dish. Fold the edges and tuck them in so the filling won't escape during baking.

Once you've filled all the pancakes, prepare the glazing.

Ingredients for the glazing:
1 egg
1–2 tbsp Greek yoghurt (or sour cream)

Whisk the egg and mix in the yoghurt/sour cream. Pour over the pancakes. Put the oven dish with the pancakes in the oven and bake for about 20 minutes.

THE COLLECTORS' SOUP

I come from a soupy culture, where soup is essentially a standard starter of every meal. Then, there's a complex soup – often with meat and vegetables – that you eat for dinner. It's a colder climate eating habit that I've carried with me all the way to the tropics.

The recipe for this soup is my mum's. I love it because it's both simple and tasty. It's a great dinner for two (more, if you're not big eaters) and an excellent lunch after a long night out.

Time needed: 30 minutes

Ingredients for 2:
3 big leeks (between 400 and 500g), cleaned, halved and sliced
3 potatoes (400g) cubed to bite-size pieces
1 tsp fresh thyme
1 tsp fresh oregano
½ stock cube
1 tbsp salt
2 tbsp oil
1 tbsp flour
a good grind of pepper

Put the cubed potatoes into 2*l* water and cook for about 15 minutes, till they're almost done. Add salt, pepper, sliced leeks, thyme, oregano and half of a stock cube.

Cook for 4–5 minutes. Heat the oil in a small pan and fry the flour for a minute or two. Add to the soup and cook for another two minutes. Serve warm.

EDDIE'S INCIDENTAL SALAD

I made this salad when trying to combine vegetables still left in our fridge with a chunk of old bread and parmesan that had to be used. The result was surprisingly tasty, so I decided to include it in this book.

It's also the kind of last-minute salad I'd expect Eddie to make. He's not the type to hop over to a farmer's market or a shop when he has perfectly good stuff in his fridge and can appropriate a few things from Becca's herb garden. The poor man hardly has time to cook with all the poker games he has lined up.

Therefore, I present to you, Eddie's Incidental Salad.

Time needed: 20 minutes

Ingredients for the salad for 2:
2 bell peppers, cubed
2 carrots, peeled and cut into tranches
160g canned chickpeas
40g shaved parmesan
2 slices dry sourdough bread, cut into bite-size pieces
1 chilli pepper, thinly sliced
2 sprigs of fresh thyme

1 tbsp fresh oregano leaves
olive oil

The dressing:
4 tbsp olive oil
1 tbsp pumpkin seed oil (if not available, substitute with another oil)
1 tbsp soy sauce
3–4 tbsp balsamic vinegar
salt and pepper to taste

Put the sourdough pieces into a pan, pour on a few table-spoons of olive oil and toast them over a low flame till they brown. Set aside. Mix the vegetables, herbs and parmesan in a salad bowl and pour over the dressing. Add the bread chunks on top and serve.

STUFFED PEPPERS

Every Balkan nation has their own version of stuffed peppers; Slovenia is no different. In this recipe, the traditional meat stuffing has been replaced with a vegetarian one.

The first version of this recipe was created by my ex-partner's mother and further improved by my own. It's one of my favourite winter dishes because it warms you up from the inside. Traditionally, it's served with potato puree, but you can also enjoy it as it is.

Time needed: 1 hour

Stuffed peppers ingredients for 2:
3 medium yellow bell peppers
75g short-grain rice, cooked till still crunchy
200ml vegetable stock
100g oats
1 egg
1 brown onion, chopped
2 garlic cloves, pressed
2 tbsp oil
1 tsp salt
a good grind of pepper

Ingredients for the tomato sauce:
3 tbsp oil
1 tbsp sugar
1 tbsp flour
1 tsp salt
650ml tomato puree

Ingredients for the potato puree:
500g potatoes
10g butter
salt, pepper
a splash of milk

First, cook the rice for about 10 minutes, till it's soft but still crunchy. Set aside to cool while you clean the peppers. Wash the peppers, cut a hole a bit bigger than the area around the stem, and take out the seeds. The opening should be big enough to fit a tablespoon and the peppers should still have some of the upper part left as you will need it to hold the stuffing inside.

Soak the cereal in the vegetable stock for 10 minutes. Drain any excess stock not absorbed by the cereal. Fry the onion in oil for about 5 minutes. Add to the cereal. Add the cooled rice, egg, salt, pepper and pressed garlic. Be sure the ingredients are cool before adding the egg. Mix well and stuff into the cleaned peppers.

Next, you make the sauce. Choose a pan with a lid that snugly fits the peppers. Heat the oil over a low to medium flame and add sugar. When the sugar begins to brown, add flour and mix to break up any lumps. When the flour browns, add tomato puree, salt and stuffed peppers. Cover and cook for about 30 minutes.

While the peppers are cooking, make the potato puree.

Peel the potatoes and cut them into cubes, roughly 1 cm big. Cover with water and cook for about 15 minutes, till they're soft. Drain, add butter and mash with a hand mixer. Add a splash of milk and salt.

Once the peppers are cooked, serve them with puree and sauce.

THE FORBIDDEN PASTA

This recipe has been among my absolute favourite comfort foods for over 20 years, ever since my friend, Nina, first whipped it up in our student dorm. Like most students at the time, I thought cooking pasta involved opening a ready-made sauce or, if none was available, a bottle of ketchup. This recipe got me hooked on cooking.

Like many good things, the formula was passed on through generations and dorms, undoubtedly improved along the way. Unfortunately, I don't know who came up with the original recipe but if you ever meet them, please express my sincere thanks. It's as delicious as it is addictive.

In our house, this pasta always wins over other options, even if they include fancy restaurants or take-outs. Whenever I offer to make it, my husband's eyes light up, then he says something like, 'Mmmm, abomination pasta.' True, the recipe boldly violates most Italian rules on pasta. It involves garlic AND onion and to add insult to injury, fish AND dairy. I prefer to call it 'The Forbidden Pasta'.

The best thing about this recipe is that it's very easy to make. It is also a recipe that hasn't found its story yet. A careful reader will

notice that the tuna pasta mentioned in 'Dash Friend' is a variation on carbonara.

Time needed: 20 minutes – more if the onion makes you cry

Ingredients for 2:
40g butter
2 brown onions, chopped (160g)
2 garlic cloves, pressed
3 cheese wedges (Laughing Cow or similar), cut into pieces
200g of canned tuna (sustainably sourced)
300–350ml cooking cream or double cream
pasta (I like to use linguine but any pasta goes)
salt and pepper to taste

Cook the pasta according to the instructions on the package.
While you wait for the water to boil, you can make the sauce.

Melt the butter over a low flame. When it starts to bubble, add
chopped onion and let it loosen for about 6 to 7 minutes. Enjoy the
sweet aroma filling your kitchen.

When the onions are yellow but not burnt, add salt, pressed
garlic and cheese. Stir with a wooden spoon till the cheese bits
melt. Add cooking cream and bring to the boil. I like to add a bit
more cream, because the sauce will thicken as it cools down. Cook
the sauce for another 2 to 3 minutes over a low flame. Add tuna
and cook for a minute, then turn it off and let it thicken. Add salt
and pepper to taste.

When the pasta is cooked, mix it with the sauce. Serve and
enjoy.

ACKNOWLEDGMENTS

This book fed my enthusiasm throughout the pandemic. As with any other book, it wouldn't have happened without the support of others.

My biggest thanks go to my husband and my first reader, the only person who reads everything I write and doesn't mind discussing the use of commas or the unfortunate destinies of my fictional characters.

I owe an enormous gratitude to my beta readers, wonderful writers and friends who saw these stories walking around in their flip flops and underpants: Jim Noonan, Patrick ten Brink, Gavin Tangen, Anastasia Coujocaru, and my bookish friends Michaela and Edith.

Very special thanks to Luka Rejec, a fellow Slovenian writer, and a friend who is also an incredible artist and game creator. His unique way of combining the cute and the sinister is only surpassed by his uncanny ability to read my mind. I'm honoured to have his illustrations alongside my stories.

A heartfelt thank you to all my writers' groups for their support and feedback, the Brussels Writers' Circle, especially Cynthia Huijgens and Colin Walsh, the kind people of the São Paulo Writers' Circle and the brilliant group of writers from our

Writers International Slack group, whom I consider my writing family.

A beam of gratitude to Jericho Writers and their wonderful community that has refreshed my writerly confidence and equipped me with the tools and knowledge to make this book a reality.

A warm thank you to my overseas friend, Margie Banin, for our chats about food and literature, which gave me the idea for one of the stories.

I'd like to thank my favourite podcast, The BBC Food Chain and its host, Emily Thomas, for providing hours of pleasure and inspiration. I cannot recommend this podcast enough.

My last thank you goes to those closest to my heart – my family: my parents, my brother and my friends. Thank you for being there and believing in me long before I did.

BEFORE YOU LEAVE

Dear Reader,

Alas, our time together has come to an end and I hope you've enjoyed reading this book. It would mean the world to me if you left an honest review.

If this book left you craving for more, there's a short story waiting for you, as dark and delicious as the ones you've read. This exclusive short story is available only to subscribers of my newsletter. You'll hear from me once a month, if I have something to share, usually good news, quirky extras and more short stories. You can unsubscribe at any point.

Shall we stay in touch? If the answer is yes, subscribe here: https://www.karmens.net/subscribe.

If the answer is no, but you'd still like to check on my work every so often, you can visit my blog or follow me on Twitter and Instagram.

Till soon.

BOOK CLUB QUESTIONS

1. How is food used in the different stories of this collection?
2. What does food reveal about the characters and their backgrounds?
3. How does food relate to a character's class and gender?
3. What other topics come up in the stories?
4. Which story was your favourite and why?
5. In what ways does food in short stories bring people together and in what ways does it put a wedge between them?
6. Which of the stories surprised you?
7. Which character do you find the most interesting and why?
8. If you could change the ending of one of the stories, which one would it be and how would you change it?
9. What did you enjoy most and least about this book, and why?
10. If you were interviewing the author, what questions would you ask her?

ABOUT THE AUTHOR

Karmen Špiljak is a Slovenian-Belgian writer with a taste for dark and twisty tales.

She writes across different genres, from suspense to horror and science fiction. Her short fiction has been awarded and anthologised. Her as yet unpublished thriller was shortlisted and received an honourable mention on 'The Black Spring Crime Fiction Prize 2020'.

She lives with her husband and two cats.
Find out more on www.karmens.net

facebook.com/karmenspiljak
twitter.com/karm3ns33ta
instagram.com/karmenseeta

MORE BY THE AUTHOR

A Perfect Flaw, an uplifting coming-of age story about identity.

LIBRARY OF EMOTIONS
A SHORT STORY

The last puddles of black rain evaporate into the tattered clouds. The instant I get out of my transport capsule, the humidity hits me like a wet cloth that sticks to the skin.

I put on my shades and tug the rim of my hood. The white sand reflects sunlight like a mirror and I don't want to start my day with a blinding headache. Not today.

The library of emotions is half an hour's walk through the dunes. It's not so much the distance as the effort needed to plod through the sand, that wears you down in the end.

For once, I want to get there before everyone with priority tickets, before the diver-hunters finish their shift and before the plantation workers get their morning break. There's about half an hour, right before they arrive, when the library is empty and I can gorge on all the emotion I want.

I think about that, as my feet sink into the warm sand. The trick is not to rush, but to let the sand settle before making the next step. Sometimes I imagine how it was before, when the world was still green and the ocean wasn't something people feared.

The waves are raging today, whiplashing at the rocks, almost as if they tried to lick the glass walls of the library. The wind starts to make the sand whirl. Only when I reach the rock and I'm standing in front of the library, do I stop to shake it off my clothes.

Then, I bring my wrist closer to the scanner, so that it reads the code on my biometric tattoo.

'Ash 12032135,' says the machine, 'state your request.'

'I request permission to enter.'

There's a beep. The door opens.

'Permission granted.'

Inside, the heavy air-conditioning reminds me of how liberating it is to breathe air at less than 40 degrees. I don't stop at the entrance screen to browse through the catalogue. It's always the same emotion I'm after, the one I need to make my life bearable.

Most people pick the popular ones like happiness, love, joy, peace. Since the time in the booths is limited, you rarely get to pick more than one. That's why I choose kindness. It brings joy, love, hope and empathy, which means I get five instead of just one. I keep this a secret. The more people choose the same emotion, the more likely the system will overload and the file will get stuck in a loop. They'll need time to find and fix the error, which could take anywhere from a couple of weeks to a couple of years. I just can't imagine living without kindness.

Before I close the doors of the booth, I put on the headphones and check that the sound works. Then, I lower myself onto the silver bar stool and turn up the volume. You don't have to close your eyes to enjoy the experience, but I prefer to. It helps me imagine what the voice is saying and makes the whole experience more intense, more real.

'Welcome back, Ash 12032135. What emotions will you play today?' the machine says.

'Kindness, please.'

'Use the remote control to navigate through the recording,' the machine says. 'After half an hour, the system will automatically switch off. You can file a request to extend the time, but in order to ensure access...'

I skip the introduction. Anyone who's ever tried to file such a request knows it's rarely approved, not unless your trauma is bigger than everyone else's. In the background, a flute starts to play.

'Kindness is an emotion invoked by acts of generosity, consideration and concern for others,' the machine says. 'In the Old World, before the Big Flood of 2053, kindness was widespread and considered to be one of the Knightly Virtues. Today...'

I fast-forward to my favourite part. The one I came for.

'Examples of kindness. Saying thank you to someone who doesn't hear it often.'

I pause and imagine a plantation, the cracked mud surrounded by glass walls, the suspended slabs that block the sunlight, but not the heat, the people, sweating in their long tunics and hats, hunched over the vegetables they're not allowed to eat. I imagine one of them looking up and wiping the sweat off his face, looking at me, checking that I'm not a mirage.

I bring them a jug of iced tea, fresh and cold, and say: 'Thanks for feeding us.'

Afterwards, I un-pause, because I don't want to be so presumptuous as to imagine a response. Besides, isn't kindness supposed to be about giving?

'Sharing an intimate gesture with a person who needs it,' the machine says.

In my mind, I'm at the docks, knee-deep in the warm ocean, waiting for the diver-hunters to end their shift. The sun is a giant orange, rising from the water, pleasant and warm, not broiling like in real life.

The seagulls start to gather and cry into the distance, as the diver-hunters emerge from under the surface, with oxygen tanks hanging over their striped uniforms. As soon as they see me, a lone figure near the shore, they clutch their nets. I'm not wearing a uniform, so they know I'm not there to check their catch, but I'm not a poacher either.

That's what I like about kindness, it inspires trust. I was wrong, it's not five emotions, but six in one. This makes me smile.

I push my thoughts aside and extend my arms to offer help with the nets. They hesitate at first, but once I help one of them, they're less reluctant. We bring out all the catch, mostly octopuses and crabs, but there's some fish, too. Once in the collection tanks, the catch will be processed for sale.

I hold this image in my head, my finger suspended above the pause button.

Un-pause.

'Be kind to someone who acts as if they don't deserve it. They need it the most,' the machine says.

I scratch my wrist. Not today. I don't deserve this yet.

Images flood my mind, the same ones that haunt my dreams, but I focus my energy to stop them from pushing forward.

Instead, I picture my colleague Lena right before I take over the shift. She's slumped in the hard plastic chair and stares at the screens.

By the time I arrive, her eyes are red from sorting out drone footage. It's my job to identify perpetrators before the forms are sent off to the Public Offences Office. I'd check the three categories from most to least serious, first critical, then suspicious and normal at the end. This way, I can go to sleep without having too many nightmares.

The hardest to process are the critical ones, the poachers, robbers, killers, people gone mad from the heat. Lena and I have seen it all. It's not a job I like, nor one I marvel at. Someone more ambitious and precise would do much better, which is why I hold on to it.

The images I held back come through. A young boy, his scruffy pants hanging loosely on his hips, as he's pulling out a net with stolen clams. The footage zooms in and locks onto the close-up. The database search begins. I can't help but hope that his name won't pop up. It does, though, because the drones got very good at reading the biometric tattoos.

Samir 21062158, twelve years old, the oldest of nine siblings. As soon as his details are confirmed, the file is sent off. All I can do is delay it by trying to correct the details. So I do. What I gain is a few minutes, perhaps hours, before the watchers at the Public Offences Office will take notice.

I'm not a good person. If I was, I'd find a better way to survive, even if by stealing food from corporations like Samir. I'm a coward, though. That's why I keep on coming to the library, hoping I'll learn how to be human. I may not deserve kindness yet, but maybe tomorrow, or the day after.

Before I know it, the machine beeps. My time in the booth is up. The door opens. There's already a queue of five people, waiting to take my space.

'The headphones,' says the first person in line, a woman of around twenty, with wide eyes and blackened fingers, probably from cleaning up after the storm.

'Oh,' I say, realising they're still around my neck. 'I'm sorry.'

I hand her the headphones and am about to leave, when she turns to me.

'What should I choose?' she whispers. 'I've only been here once before.'

I size her up, the dark hollows under her eyes, the reddish marks on her neck where the sand has irritated the skin. Behind her, someone grunts. I consider speeding things up by saying one of the usual things, like 'depends on what you need' or 'the most popular ones are at the top', but her pleading gaze makes me pause.

So I lean closer, till I can see the grains of sand in her hair and smell the rain and the beach rubble on her clothes.

'Choose kindness,' I say. 'There's nothing better.'

She pauses, perhaps unsure if I'm pulling her leg.

'Trust me,' I say. 'You won't regret it.'

The muscles on her face relax. She smiles. She catches a strand of loose hair and coaxes it back behind her ear.

'Will you move on? Haven't got all day,' the next person in the queue shouts out.

'Thank you,' she says and rests her hand on my shoulder, then slowly, as if we had all the time in the world, she pulls me into a hug.

I freeze.

Layers of yesterdays, hours of surveillance footage, the submitted offences, they all peel off and melt into water. Tears pour down my cheeks, hot and sticky. I don't stop them. Instead, I put my arms around the woman and return the hug.

This story has won the dystopian short story competition in 'Writing Magazine' and was published in March 2021.

Lightning Source UK Ltd.
Milton Keynes UK
UKHW010734121021
392080UK00003B/540